No one can accuse author Robert Thornhill of not being relevant.

Fast-paced and humorous, the reader will find himself racing through the pages to see how Walt and his friends once again bring down all the bad people and restore justice to their corner of the world.

The newest mystery comedy in the Walt Williams series, *Lady Justice and the Assassin*, mixes the topical concerns of a still sluggish economy; the middle class being driven into poverty; and the perceived trampling of civil liberties, in particular those protected by the 2nd Amendment. The story combines the forces of two groups to hatch a plot to assassinate the president and vice-president.

The man chosen for the task, normally a patriotic American who never even had a speeding ticket, is presented the opportunity to reclaim all his possessions and set his family onto the path of solvency by doing just one small task for the alliance: shoot the president. Will he do it? Additionally, Walt and his partner, Ox, deal with daily crime and life in Kansas City, MO., recruitment for members in a black gang and the strange shaving of pedigree dogs.

The combination of these simultaneous cases makes for fun reading. This book has all the old stand-by characters that readers have come to love in the earlier editions. Christina Jones, Independence, MO.

****

The author, Robert Thornhill provides all the elements to enjoy when you pick up one of his books in the Lady Justice Mystery/Comedy series. You get to laugh and enjoy the mystery, excitement, and suspense as he draws you into the plot each and every time. In this one, you'll be amazed how much you find yourself fighting for the underdog, Henry Martin.

Yet, you are also able to empathize with how something like this could happen to someone in such desperate despair. In today's economics, Henry Martin would not be the only one tempted by such a deal. Will his conscience save him?

Lady Justice and the Assassin is about politics, prejudice and guns (the second amendment). The plot thickens as two organizations with different beliefs; the Aryan Brotherhood and the Ozark Militia, are plotting the assassination the President of the United States!

The lengths they go to are unbelievable.

Walt Williams is a classic old time cop, one who finds himself in the right place at the wrong time. You fall in love with his friends! They add the right amount of humor to the story to keep you turning the page.

As this is going on, Walt and his partner are trying to keep a young boy from joining the neighborhood gang known as the 'Vipers'. The boy has skills they need and Rashon, the gang leader, goes to serious lengths to persuade him to join.

Once again, I found this book a good read and

nice addition to the series. I can't get enough of them
and wait patiently for the next one to arrive!
Mary Stanhope, Article Write Up.

****

Robert Thornhill hits it once again with
controversial and serious topics.
Walt's first assignment is to catch a person
who is shaving the fur off of purebred dogs. He also
has to save one of his friends as two opposing gangs
are at war, and he faces one of his most challenging
cases of his career: to protect the President of the
United States. To Walt's surprise, he finds himself
trying to stop an assassin who is determined to kill
the president at any cost.
Robert Thornhill is an author to watch. He
knows how to blend humor and serious topics
together to create the perfect all night read.
Sheri Wilkinson, Princeton, IL.

****

What Readers Are Saying

About The Lady Justice Series

Look out Stephanie Plum! I think Walt and his gang are going to give you a run for the money. I think I enjoy Walt and his gang more than I do the Stephanie Plum series. Can't wait for the next book in the series. Thanks again Mr. Thornhill for such an awesome series! Gail, Novi, MI.

****

A humorous mystery novel that made me think of Janet Evanovich`s books. I had been immediately attracted to the book by the title and cover. The blurb made me know it was going to be an adventure with plenty of murder and mystery told in a light-hearted way. I love the "noir" type of book. Sherry, Pensacola, FL.

****

Robert Thornhill is my go to author for a mood elevation! This 12th book in the Lady Justice series has the same great blend of mystery, suspense and humor. The subject matter is current and thought provoking without being in your face. I love Walt and the gang! Heather, Neosho, Mo.

****

I love the mix of mystery with the humor. I highly recommend this book to every mystery lover and to anyone else who is thinking of reading something different for a change of pace. Linda, Waynesville, NC.

****

This book is a hoot to read! It is also refreshingly delightful to have an "elderly" hero! Annie, Saint Paul, MN.

****

A well-executed murder mystery that has the elements of a dark comedy - light reading with dark, eerie overtones. Amy, Indie Reader Review

****

I found it refreshing that the characters of the series are past middle age. The author showed that just because somebody is older they still are able to kick butt. Conny, Puyallup, WA.

****

Robert Thornhill is a great author and this is a great series! If you haven't already discovered this author and this series, there's no time like the present. You don't know what you're missing! Cathy, Rib Lake, WI.

LADY JUSTICE

AND THE

ASSASSIN

A Walt Williams
Mystery/Comedy Novel

ROBERT THORNHILL

LADY JUSTICE AND THE ASSASSIN

PROLOGUE

In the dimly lit room, the president's image filled the TV screen.

"Real reform means fixing the legal immigration system to cut waiting periods and attract the highly skilled entrepreneurs and engineers that will help create jobs and grow our economy.

"In other words, we know what needs to be done. And as we speak, bipartisan groups in both chambers are working diligently to draft a bill, and I applaud their efforts. So let's get this done. Send me a comprehensive immigration reform bill in the next few months, and I will sign it right away. America will be better for it.

"I know this is not the first time this country has debated how to reduce gun violence, but this time is different. Overwhelming majorities of Americans -- Americans who believe in the Second Amendment -- have come together around common sense reform, like background checks that will make it harder for criminals to get their hands on a gun.

"Senators of both parties are working together on tough new laws to prevent anyone from buying guns for resale to criminals. Police chiefs are asking our help to get weapons of war and massive ammunition magazines off our streets, because these police chiefs, they're tired of seeing their guys and gals being outgunned. Each of these proposals

deserves a vote in Congress."

Brant Jaeger switched off the TV and slammed the remote against the wall. "Damn! There it is! This president is determined to make our country a socialist state. The number of people on the public dole increases every day. Hell, there's just no incentive to work anymore. Why would someone bust his butt when Uncle Sam is willing to foot the bill?

"If his immigration bill passes, it would instantly legalize eleven million illegal immigrants living here now.

"Our country is already full of illegal aliens taking jobs away from Americans and now he wants to make it easier for immigrants to get into the country and become citizens. Did you know that in 1960, whites made up 85% of the population, but that figure has dropped to 64% and it is projected that by 2050, whites will be a minority in their *OWN COUNTRY* with 47% of the population?"

Terrance Cobb's reaction to this outburst was a mixture of amusement and concern. "Looks like your Aryan Revolution is fighting a losing battle."

"What about you and your Ozark Militia, Cobb?" Jaeger retorted. "If the King has his way, you'll be handing over your AK-47's before the year is over."

The glint of amusement in Cobb's eyes turned to steely resolve.

"Ever heard the statement, 'I'll give you my gun when you pry it from my cold, dead hands'?

Well that's not just rhetoric bullshit --- that's our creed and it's ingrained in every last man in my militia."

Jaeger narrowed his eyes. "Looks like we have something in common, Cobb. There's another statement, 'The enemy of my enemy is my friend'. I never imagined that the Aryan Brotherhood would mingle with a bunch of scruffy hillbillies from the Ozarks, but it seems we have a common foe and it might be in our best interests to work together."

"And it never occurred to me that the militia would give the time of day to Nazi skin-heads, but I can see your point. What do you have in mind?"

"I think that it's obvious. The current administration is a cancer in our American way of life. It is weakening the fabric of our nation from within, and like any malignancy, it must be removed if the body is to survive.

"The administration successfully fought off impeachment, so now, if our country is to prosper, it is time for more drastic measures!"

CHAPTER 1

A weary and disconsolate Henry Martin tossed the mail onto the table and slumped into a chair.

Marsha Martin sensed that her husband's search for employment had not been successful.

After twelve years in the marketing department at Majestic Enterprises, Henry had been let go when the company relocated its manufacturing plant to Mexico. His unemployment benefit had expired and his daily forays into human resource offices throughout the city had yielded nothing. He had submitted his resume to dozens of firms online without so much as a response.

Marsha sat beside him and took his hand. "No luck, sweetie?"

Martin shook his head. "I just don't get it. I can't even get a job flipping burgers at Micky D's. Some kid with a lip stud and an earring that can't even make change correctly is behind the counter at the cash register. I have a MBA and twelve years on the job and they won't even look at me because I'm 'over qualified'. Something is *VERY* wrong with this country."

"Maybe tomorrow will be better. Somebody out there has to be looking for a man with your qualifications."

Martin picked up the mail and began thumbing through the envelopes.

"Bills, bills and more bills. This one is

marked 'final notice'. It won't be long before we're hearing from the collection companies."

They heard the door slam shut and twelve-year-old Billy burst into the room.

"Mom, Dad, look at this," he said with excitement, handing them a form letter. "Tryouts for Pop Warner football are this weekend. Can I try out? Pleeeeease!"

Martin looked at the form and the first thing that caught his eye was the enrollment fee --- $200.00.

"I don't think so, Son."

"But, Dad!"

"You know how your mother and I feel about contact football." The last thing he wanted to tell his son was that he couldn't play because his dad was a failure. "Even NFL players are having second thoughts because of all the concussions and head injuries. We'll talk about baseball in the spring."

Billy hung his head and slumped off to his room. "I never get to do anything!" he mumbled.

Marsha saw the tears well up in her husband's eyes. "Even if we could afford it, you were right. It's just too dangerous."

"That's not the point, is it?" he said, choking back his emotion. "It could have been anything --- music lessons, swimming --- and we still would have told him 'no'. What kind of dad am I?"

"You're the best dad any boy could ever want. We're just going through a rough patch. We'll make it --- somehow."

Henry picked up another letter. "Marcus-Pinkerton Law Firm. This can't be good."

He tore open the envelope and Marsha could see from the anguish on her husband's face that it was not good news.

Henry tossed the letter onto the table. "I didn't think it could get any worse, but there it is."

"What now?"

"The mortgage company said they would work with us, but apparently they've had a change of heart. This is a foreclosure notice. Our home will be sold on the courthouse steps in sixty days unless we can pay the note off in full. We're going to be homeless."

Marsha had tried to put on a brave front for her husband, but this latest blow was more than she could bear. She fell into Henry's arms and sobbed uncontrollably.

He held her close. He wanted to cry with her, but all he could feel was emptiness. The shock had drained him of all emotion.

When Marsha's sobs had subsided, he held her at arm's length.

"You have to go --- you and Billy."

"What are you talking about? Go where? We can't leave you. We won't!"

"Call your parents. They have plenty of room in their basement for the two of you."

"But ---!"

"Think about it, Marsha. Think about Billy. I don't want him seeing the only home he has ever known taken from us. There are other families out there living in their cars. I don't want that for the two of you. He won't even have to change schools. I know your parents will help."

"But what will you do?"

"I'll stay here as long as I can. I have sixty days to do something with all of the stuff that we've accumulated over the years. I'll sell what we don't absolutely have to have and use the money to rent a storage shed for what we want to keep. I'll keep looking for work. Maybe something will turn up. I'll come by to see you every day. I promise."

"There must be some other way ---!"

"Marsha, I need for you to be brave. You said it yourself --- we're going through a rough patch, but if you stick with me, we'll make it through all of this."

"I promised I would be your wife for better or for worse. I guess this is the worse part. Just tell me what I need to do."

"That's my girl. We'll figure this out somehow. After all, this is America, the land of opportunity. I just know that something will come along."

CHAPTER 2

My name is Walt Williams. I'm a sixty-nine-year-old cop and just happy to be alive.

For the second time in less than a year, I was nearly blown to bits by a Mexican drug cartel's grenade launcher. Miraculously, I escaped both times, most recently because of the sacrifice of two old gentlemen from the Whispering Hills Retirement Village.

My partner, Ox, and I are just regular beat cops. We're supposed to do simple stuff like serving warrants, crowd control and the occasional domestic disturbance, but somehow, the fickle finger of fate has poked us into cases way above our pay grade.

With the demise of Hector Corazon and his fellow druggies, we were happy to be back on our regular beat, which on most morning includes a stop at Dunkin Donuts or Krispy Kreme. This morning was no exception.

Ox has a sweet tooth and apparently a hollow leg as well. He can pack a lot of groceries into his 6'2", two hundred and twenty pound body.

The box that he carried out of the shop was large enough to hold a half dozen of the tasty treats.

"Cream-filled as usual?" I inquired as he climbed into the driver's seat.

"Nope. I'm living dangerously today. Thought I'd change things up --- went with powdered sugar --- you know --- like the little mini-donuts that come six in a package from the grocery store --- only these suckers are full sized! They smell great!" he said opening the box and taking a big sniff.

Unlike icing which clings to the pastry like glue, powdered sugar is susceptible to the slightest breeze. I winced as I watched him inhale a snootful of the white confection.

He realized immediately that he had made a tactical error. His eyes grew wide as he felt the sugar fill his sinuses.

We both knew what was coming but we were powerless to stop it.

I turned away just as the sneeze exploded from his lungs. Unfortunately, the force of the blast was directed into the open box on his lap.

Powdered sugar spewed into the air, filling the cruiser like snowfall on a winter's day. Our blue uniforms, fresh from the cleaners, were now ghastly pale.

"Opps! Sorry!" he said, wiping the white dust from the steering wheel.

I could only imagine what the guy in the next car was thinking when two cops climbed out of their cruiser looking like 'Pig-Pen' from the Charlie Brown cartoons.

Fifteen minutes later, after dusting off our uniforms and wiping down the interior of the cruiser, we were ready for duty.

"Donut?" Ox asked, offering me the box.

"Ummm, thanks, but I'll pass," I replied, remembering the sneeze that had sent the powder into orbit.

Just then the radio came to life.

"Car 54. What's your twenty?"

I almost said 'Dunkin Donuts', but then I reconsidered.

"We're on Main, just north of the Plaza."

"Proceed to 5421 Oak. The resident has reported a break-in."

"On our way."

"What are you and Judy up to this weekend?" I asked as Ox headed south on Main through the Plaza.

"Nothing yet. Keeping our options open. What did you have in mind?"

The last time Maggie and I double dated with Ox and Judy, the girls were less than impressed. We had taken them to the Burrito Bandito in the smelly City Market so that we could keep an eye on the druggies operating a fruit stand next door. Afterward, we had been informed in no uncertain terms that we owed them big time and that an evening of fine dining was somewhere in our near future.

Ox and I don't do fine dining.

"Maggie keeps reminding me that I still owe her for that City Market thing. It's kind of like a toothache --- I don't want to go to the dentist, but I know I'll have to eventually so I might as well get it over with."

"Judy's been on my case too. Think we ought to bite the bullet?"

We had just pulled up in front of the Oak address.

"We're here. Let's discuss our options at lunch."

We knocked on the door and were met by a very prim and proper matron that appeared to be in her sixties.

"Good morning, Ma'am. I'm Officer George Wilson and this is my partner, Walt Williams. I understand you've had some problems."

She held the door open and stepped aside. "I'm Abigail Fitzhugh and yes, we certainly have."

We figured from the address that the owners would be well off and we weren't disappointed. The home was decorated with massive furnishings, and antique pieces were perched on every available surface.

"What seems to be the problem?" Ox inquired. "The dispatcher mentioned something about a break-in."

"Let me show you something," she said, reaching for a photo in an ornate gilded frame. "This is Lazarus. We call him Lazzie."

Ox took the frame and we found ourselves staring at the photo of a hairy little dog that looked like a miniature yak. On closer inspection, his face bore a striking resemblance to Chewbacca, the Wookiee in the *Star Wars* movies.

"Nice pooch," Ox observed.

I saw Mrs. Fitzhugh stiffen. "Lazzie is not a pooch! He is a pure bred Lhasa Apso!"

"A what?"

It was obvious that Mrs. Fitzhugh was

appalled by our lack of canine breeding.

"Lhasa Apso! They were bred in Tibet by Buddhist monks. Lhasa is the capital city of Tibet and Apso means bearded. We had him flown into the United States directly from a Buddhist monastery."

"Very impressive," I said, attempting to smooth her ruffled feathers. "Was Lazzie taken during the break-in?"

"Thankfully, no, but he was certainly disgraced."

I couldn't imagine how a dog could be disgraced. I was about to find out.

"Let me show you. Lazzie! Come!"

Moments later, a scrawny pink creature that looked nothing like the regal Lazarus poked his head around the corner.

"Come here, baby," she cooed. "Come to mama."

The pitiful creature crept toward its mistress with its tail tucked between his legs.

She picked him up and held him at arms length.

"This is my poor Lazarus. Someone broke into my home and shaved my dog!"

Ox and I were speechless.

In Ox's twenty-plus years on the force, this was probably his first dog-shaving case. I know that it was a first for me.

"Well, what are you going to do?" Mrs. Fitzhugh asked, indignantly.

"Let's start with the break-in," I said. "Was

there a forced entry?"

"My husband and I were at a benefit dinner last evening," she said leading us through the house. "When we returned we found this," she said, pointing to the back door.

A pane of glass in the door had been broken, giving the intruder access to the deadbolt lock.

"Was anything taken from your home?" Ox asked.

"Nothing! We looked in every room. Nothing was taken. We have silver, jewelry, a wall safe, but the only thing we found was poor Lazarus."

"Can you think of any reason why someone would shave your dog?" I asked. "Was his fur valuable?"

"Of course not. The perpetrator didn't even bother to take it. Here let me show you."

She picked up a gallon zip-lock bag filled with hair.

"I couldn't bear to part with it."

I wondered if she was planning to glue it back on, but I figured I'd better not go there.

"Can you think of any possible reason why someone would do this?" Ox asked. "Revenge --- a grudge --- trouble with neighbors?"

"No," she said, shaking her head. "Nothing like that. We get along well with everyone."

"Then I'd say you were pretty lucky that you escaped with nothing more serious than a shaved dog," Ox observed.

That was the wrong thing to say.

"Officer! Apparently you don't comprehend the devastating psychological trauma that has been inflicted on my poor Lazarus. Imagine a peacock that has been stripped of his plumage --- a magnificent elephant whose tusks have been cut away. It will take months of therapy for my pet and he may never be the same."

"Sorry, ma'am," Ox apologized. "I didn't intend to minimize your situation. It's just that many home invasions turn out far worse for the homeowners."

"So I ask again. What are you going to do?"

"We'll get the lab guys out here to dust for prints. Maybe they'll come up with something, and if you can think of anything else that might help us, please call," Ox said handing her his card.

Lazarus started squirming in Mrs. Fitzhugh's arms.

"Poor thing. He needs to go out."

We followed her to the front door. She placed him on the ground and he ran to the far corner of the yard.

"He's so humiliated," Mrs. Fitzhugh moaned, as we watched the pitiful creature do his business.

A squirrel perched on a branch above the dog was chattering away. It sounded like he was laughing at the once regal pooch. I almost felt sorry for him --- almost.

As we headed back to the cruiser, I heard Mrs. Fitzhugh's plaintive cry, "Lazzie! Come home!"

CHAPTER 3

The old warehouse in the West Bottoms had once been a small manufacturing operation, but the previous owners had long since closed the doors and moved to a country where wages were cheap and labor unions were non-existent.

It had set vacant for years until it was rented by ABC Ltd., a company cloaked in secrecy.

In the drafty hall that had been converted into a meeting room, Brant Jaeger, a representative of the company, sat across the table from Terrance Cobb, the Commander of the Ozark Militia.

"Nice digs, Brant. Looks like the Brotherhood is really living high on the hog."

"Cut the crap, Cobb. Did you come here to insult me or are we going to do business together?"

"Calm down, Brant. I'm just a country boy havin' a little fun. If we're gonna work together, you gotta lighten up."

"Sorry," Jaeger replied, backing down. "What did your people have to say?"

"Like you said at our last meeting, 'the enemy of my enemy is my friend', but I think William Shakespeare said it best in *The Tempest*, 'Misery acquaints a man with strange bedfellows'. We have concluded that our two organizations have a common goal --- the removal of that heretic from office."

"Shakespeare! I would never have guessed that you were a student of the classics."

"Don't underestimate us just because we

prefer to live in the hills and shoot the food for our table. It wouldn't be wise. Now if we're finished with the verbal jousting, exactly what is your organization suggesting?"

"I think it is obvious," Jaeger replied. "The only course of action left to us is assassination. It is a drastic course, but necessary if we are to protect our Second Amendment rights and keep our society from being further polluted by interlopers from foreign shores. Drastic times call for drastic measures."

"Even if you are successful, what have you accomplished? The president's successor is a carbon copy and supports the same agenda."

"Precisely! That's why it must be a duel assassination. We will eliminate both at the same time. In the current line of succession, the presidency would then fall to the Speaker of the House of Representatives, a member of the opposing party and a man more sympathetic to our mutual causes."

"A double assassination! It has never been done! Are we embarking on a noble cause or a fool's errand?"

"Maybe the militia doesn't have the stomach for such an enterprise. Maybe you are all content to hide in your hills and rattle your swords. To quote your Shakespeare, 'Much ado about nothing'!"

Cobb's eyes narrowed, "We are sworn to take up arms against any threat to our Republic, either foreign or domestic. If you question our resolve, remember what fate befell your precious Hitler."

Anger flashed across Jaeger's face, then

quickly faded. "Peace, Brother. We have a common foe and we must stand together. Truce?"

Cobb smiled. "Truce. Am I to assume that you will want a pair of sharpshooters? We have some remarkable marksmen in our ranks."

"No, that won't be necessary."

"And why not? You won't find finer marksmen anywhere."

"I'm sure that's true, Cobb, and that's part of the problem."

"I don't follow."

"Homeland Security," Jaeger replied. "Your organization as well as ours is on their watch list. Why do you think we meet in a building such as this? We have relocated three times in this year alone. Every week, we have a man scour the entire building for bugs planted by our fascist government. They will eventually find us again and we will move on. It's a game we play.

"Any overt action by either of our organizations will bring the wrath of Homeland Security crashing down upon us. Using their powers under the Patriot Act, they can do pretty much anything they want with impunity. What chance would your militia have against government drones laying waste to your forest encampment?"

"I see your point. What do you have in mind?"

"John Q. Public. The man on the street --- a law-abiding citizen with no police record or ties to questionable organizations. They can't watch everyone, and our assassin will be from the ranks of those they least suspect."

"Why would a man agree to such a despicable act --- an act that would most likely lead to his death or to life imprisonment at the least?"

"Men do despicable acts every day, for revenge, power, lust, money. We simply need to find men with a powerful motive, provide the means, and the act will follow. I believe we have found such men."

"Sounds like you have things pretty well mapped out. What do you need from my militia?"

"Money --- and lots of it. The men we have in mind need money for their families. For some men, their most powerful instinct is to provide and protect their families. If they believe that can be accomplished, even at the risk of their own lives, they will act."

"What makes you think the members of my militia have that kind of money? We're just common folks, not millionaires."

"Where does your militia get their AK-47's and ammunition? The gun manufacturers are in the same boat as us. If this administration gets its way, their profits will tumble. You may not have deep pockets, but they do, and I'm willing to bet that you know who to talk to.

"We have powerful interests that are sympathetic to our cause and are willing to make a financial commitment. If you can get your gun manufacturers on board, we can put this thing together and get our country back on the right course. Are you in?"

"I'll make some calls. You're a crazy bastard, but this just might work!"

"So did you talk to Judy about going out for dinner tomorrow night?" I asked as we headed to our cruiser.

"Sure did! She asked me what I'd done wrong this time. Can you believe it? What about you?"

"Pretty much the same reaction. Why is it so hard to believe that two guys just want to take their girls to a nice dinner out of the goodness of their hearts?"

"Maybe because it doesn't happen very often. They're not dummies. Judy said that she'd talk to Maggie and let us know."

We always get in trouble when they 'confer'. Maggie already ruled out Mel's and Denny's, but we knew that would happen.

We had just gotten underway when the radio crackled. "Car 54, didn't you guys take that call with the shaved dog yesterday?"

"That's affirmative."

"Well, we have another one and the captain wants you to take it."

"Another shaved dog?"

"That's what the caller said. The address is

8712 Summit in Western Hills."

"What's with this 'mad groomer'?" Ox asked, hanging up the mike. "Why would anyone break into homes just to shave a dog? It doesn't make any sense!"

"I can see breaking in to steal a dog --- some of them are quite valuable," I replied, "or maybe to get rid of one. Some of them are obnoxious little yappers, but I don't get the shaving thing either."

The home on Summit was much like the one the day before --- the owners were obviously not hurting for money.

Ox's knock was met by a woman in her fifties that looked like she was trying to recapture thirty. Her hair was bleached blonde and piled high on her head. Her knockers screamed silicone and her face had probably been under the knife more than Joan Rivers. I think she was trying to smile at us, but it was difficult to tell with all of the Botox.

"I'm Edith Barksdale. Thank you for responding so quickly. Claude and I are absolutely beside ourselves. This has been a shock to both of us."

"So Claude is your dog?" Ox asked.

"Oh, my goodness no. Claude is my husband. Alphonse Beauregard is our Bichon Frise. We call him Alfie." She gave her head a little tilt. "He is a direct descendant from the court of Henry III of France."

We both nodded like we knew what the hell she was talking about.

"Tell us what happened," Ox said.

"Claude and I had dinner with friends at the Country Club last evening. When we returned, we discovered that our home and our pet had been violated."

"By 'violated' you mean shaved?" Ox ventured.

"Let me show you," she said, retrieving a photo that was nestled among several trophies that I assumed Alphonse had won.

The dog looked like a little white powder puff. His body was covered with curly hair that had been sculptured so that he looked like one of those chia pets that you see on late night infomercials.

"Cute," Ox said. "Where is little Alfie now?"

"Hiding in disgrace!" she replied dramatically. "I'll see if I can find him."

"Great," I said. "While you're looking, could you show us where the perp entered your home?"

A back door into the garage had been jimmied with a crowbar. The door from the garage to the kitchen had not been locked.

When Edith returned, she was holding something that looked more like a rat than the regal descendant of a royal court.

The poor thing was shivering. He had probably never been naked before.

For just a moment, I could feel his embarrassment. My mind flashed back to that recurring dream we all have, where we find ourselves in the supermarket in our underwear.

"Any idea who would do this or why?" I asked.

"None whatsoever. Claude and I have racked our brains trying to make sense of all this."

"By any chance do you know Abigail Fitzhugh?" Ox asked.

"No, I'd don't believe that I do. Why do you ask?"

"The same thing happened to her dog yesterday."

"Oh, no! How horrible. So this is the work of a serial shaver?"

I hadn't really thought of it in those terms, but she was right, and if indeed it was the work of a serial shaver, there would be more pet peelings.

"I just wish you could talk," Edith said, pressing the pitiful beast against her ample, store-bought cleavage. "Then you could tell us what it's all about, Alfie."

For the second time in two days, we summoned the lab boys to dust for prints.

We resumed our patrol, wondering when and where the defiler of regal dogs would strike again.

CHAPTER 4

Brant Jaeger picked up the phone. "Yes."

"This is Cobb. I have what you're looking for."

"Not on the phone. Someone might be listening. One hour --- same place as before."

"I'll be there."

"I've got to hand it to you, Jaeger. You were right on. It didn't take much arm twisting to get the gun boys on board, but it might take a few days to get the cash."

"Let me guess. They're going to route the funds through several offshore dummy corporations so that if anything goes south with the operation their hands will be clean."

Cobb smiled. "You had it figured all along, didn't you?"

"That's what I would have done. Anyway, it doesn't matter. Now that we know the money is available, I can make the first contact with our mark. I don't expect him to say 'yes' right away, but he'll come around. His family is desperate."

"I'll let you know when the money has cleared," Cobb said. "In the meantime, do you need anything else from the militia?"

"As soon as we have our assassin on board,

I'll need for you to check him out. We can't expect a guy that has spent the last twelve years sitting behind a desk to be a sharpshooter --- especially with a handgun. I expect that he'll need a week or more at that Ozark encampment of yours to become proficient enough to pull this off."

"If he's got two good eyes and his hands don't shake, we'll make a shooter out of him. By the way, you've only mentioned one guy. Who's taking care of the vice president?"

"Don't worry about that," Jaeger replied. "The VP will be on the West Coast when all of this comes down. We have an organization in California similar to yours handling that end of things. The more we can keep the operation compartmentalized, the safer we all will be if something goes wrong."

"Makes sense. Let me know when your boy is on board."

The house was deathly quiet as Henry Martin opened the box that held their wedding album.

The only sound was the ticking of the old mantel clock that had belonged to his grandparents. He silently wondered what would become of the treasured heirloom when the house was gone.

As he thumbed through the pages of the album, he reflected on that time so many years ago.

Everything was so perfect then. He had just graduated with his MBA and landed the job at Majestic Enterprises. His first paycheck was all the encouragement that he needed to ask Marsha to be his wife. He had promised her that he would take care of her forever.

A tear rolled down his cheek and landed on the photo of them standing at the alter exchanging vows.

"*How*," he thought, "*could things change so drastically?*"

Little Billy had come along a year later. He had been so proud when he opened the savings account for his son's college tuition. That account had been emptied months ago to pay utility bills.

He looked around the basement storage room. His whole life was stored away in the boxes that were stacked in neat rows. He had to decide what to save and what to throw away, and he just wasn't up to the heartbreaking task.

The sound of the telephone interrupted his melancholy musings. His first impulse was to ignore it --- probably bill collectors harassing him for a payment --- but it might be Marsha.

"Hello," he said cautiously.

"Hello, Mr. Martin."

Henry nearly dropped the phone. The voice coming over the line had obviously been altered electronically. He had heard voice enhancers on many mystery programs on TV, but he had never experienced one in real life.

"Y-Y-Yes. This is Henry Martin. Who is this?"

"At this point in time, you can just call me Max. I have a proposition that I think will interest you."

"A proposition? What kind of proposition?"

"First, let me tell you what I know about your situation. You lost your position at Majestic Enterprises several months ago and haven't found new employment. Your benefits have run their course and in sixty days your home with be auctioned on the courthouse steps."

"How could you know all of that?"

"Please Mr. Martin. This is the electronic age. You of all people should know that. Everything about everyone is available somewhere. One just has to know where to look. Now, to make matters even worse, your wife, Marsha, and Billy have had to take shelter with her parents --- on Brookside Boulevard, I believe."

"Look, Max --- or whatever your name is, my family is none of your business and if you ---!"

"Calm down, Henry. I'm not here to threaten your family. I'm here to help. Now are you interested in hearing my proposition?"

His first impulse was to hang up, but curiosity got the better of him. "Go ahead. I'm listening."

"Very wise choice, Henry. If my calculations are correct, a quarter of a million dollars would set your family up very nicely. It would pay off the remaining balance on your home, clear out the balances on those pesky credit cards that you have maxed out and maybe even be enough to replace the funds in little Billy's college savings account."

Henry was speechless.

"I suppose that you're wondering what you would have to do to earn that kind of money? I would be too. Before I tell you, I want you to think very carefully about your family and what lies ahead for them. What options do you have to pull them back from the brink of disaster?"

Silence.

"That's what I thought, Henry. Now are you interested in hearing my proposition or should I just hang up?"

"I'm listening."

"It's really quite simple. You have but one thing to do to earn that rather large sum of money and save your family."

"And what would that be?"

"Assassinate the President of the United States."

Henry couldn't believe what he was hearing. During the conversation, he had imagined several scenarios, but nothing like this.

"Are you crazy? What makes you think that I would ever even consider such a heinous act?"

"Because, Henry, you are a desperate man and desperate men do desperate things --- especially to save their families. I know you're not a murderer or a sociopath. If you were, we wouldn't be having this conversation.

"Think about this. If an intruder broke into your home and threatened Marsha and Billy, and you had the means to end that threat, would you hesitate?"

"Of course not. But this is different."

"How is this different? Your family has been put in harm's way by a government that sent your job to Mexico. You are competing with thousands of others for the few jobs that are available. The government gave billions to bail out the banks, but hasn't spent a dime helping a hard working man like yourself save his home. I could go on, but you're a sharp guy. You get the picture. All we're asking you to do is eliminate the threat to your family."

"I - I - I could never do that. It's just not right. I'm no assassin!"

"Henry, I know this is a lot to digest. I'm not asking you to make a decision right this minute. Think about it. Think about what a quarter of a million dollars could do for your family. I'll give you this number. Just so you know, it is a burner phone and untraceable, but you probably figured that already. You might also think how silly you would sound, going to the police and telling them that some guy called and offered you two hundred and fifty grand to kill the president. Think about your family, Henry. This is your ticket out of this mess. I'll be waiting for your call."

The line went dead.

Henry remained motionless for several minutes, replaying the conversation in his mind.

"Who was this guy? Was it just a crank call? A horrible prank? A foreign government? Al-Qaeda?"

It really didn't matter. There was no way that he would ever consider such a despicable act.

He climbed the stairs and turned off the basement lights.

As he walked through the kitchen, he passed the door casing where marks measuring Billy's height had been made every year on his birthday.

In a few months, these marks, precious to his family, would be painted over by some new family and lost forever.

He stood in the silence of the lonely house, his heart aching for his family, his mind envisioning things he never thought possible.

CHAPTER 5

Captain Short laid the sheaf of papers on his desk. "Nothing! The crime lab boys couldn't find a fingerprint other than the owners at either location. No evidence of any kind. Have you come up with anything?"

Ox shook his head. "The owners are as baffled as we are. We can't come up with any logical motive why anyone would break into a home just to shave a dog --- unless maybe we're dealing with some kind of wacko. They really don't need a reason."

"Any connection between the two families?"

"Not that we have found," I replied. "They live in different parts of the city, run in different social circles and neither remembers ever meeting the other."

"You can go back to your regular patrol unless --- ." At that moment, the Captain's intercom buzzed.

"Captain Short. Call on line three."

The Captain motioned for us to wait while he took the call. After a brief conversation, he hung up and gave us a puzzled look. "Forget the regular patrol. There's been another dog shaving. This time it's a Labradoodle. Stop by my secretary's desk on your way out. She'll give you the address. Bring me something this time."

While the two previous shavings had taken place in well-to-do neighborhoods, the address of the latest assault on our furry friends was in a blue-collar part of the city.

"I don't get it," Ox said. "Lhasa Apso, Bichon Frise and now a Labradoodle. Whatever happened to plain old dogs? Doesn't anyone own a Collie or a Cocker Spaniel anymore? Seems like the perp is only interested in the more exotic breeds and he certainly isn't interested in shaving mutts."

"Good observation," I replied. "There has to be some connection between these dogs that we just haven't seen yet."

We pulled up in front of a modest, but well maintained two-story home.

Ox looked at the case printout. "Owner's name is Morton Baughman. I can't wait to hear his story."

We knocked and a thirty-something guy in a sweat suit opened the door.

After introductions, Ox got right to the point. "Your dog. What happened?"

"In order for you to get the full impact of our situation, I need to show you this," he said, grabbing two photos from his coffee table."

"That's a dog?" Ox asked. "Looks like a lion!"

"Exactly!" Baughman said. "That's Charlie.

He lives in Virginia and he's very well known to the local police. His owner, Chris Painter, had him groomed to look like a lion and he's become quite a celebrity. He even has his own Facebook page with over a thousand friends."

"Interesting," I said, "but what's that have to do with our current situation?"

He handed us another photo. "This is my dog Duke. The Duke of Earl, actually. We had him groomed just like Charlie. Cost me two hundred bucks."

The dogs in the two photos could have been lion brothers.

"And now?" I asked, already knowing the answer.

"And now it's gone --- all of it --- along with my two hundred bucks. And that's not the worst. Let me show you something."

He grabbed a remote off the coffee table and pushed some buttons. The disk started playing, the TV screen lit up and Duke was standing in regal anticipation of something that was happening off screen. A few seconds later, the old 50's song, *Duke of Earl*, by Gene Chandler could be heard. As soon as the song started, Duke was on his hind legs twirling to the music.

Duke --- Duke --- Duke --- Duke of Earl --- Duke --- Duke. As I walk through this world, nothing can stop the Duke of Earl.

Duke danced until the song ended and eagerly waited for the treat from his owner that he knew would be coming.

"That's really cool," I said, earnestly. "That song is one of my favorites. So what's the problem?"

"Let me show you," he said, leading us into the kitchen.

Lying on a rug with his head resting on his paws was the once regal, now shaved, Duke of Earl. The look in his eyes could only be described as sad and forlorn.

"Here, Duke," Baughman coaxed. "Come to Daddy." He held out a treat. The dog looked but never moved.

"Now watch this," he said, flipping a switch on a boom box.

Gene Chandler's classic song filled the room, but poor Duke never moved.

Baughman flipped off the boom box. He's been like this ever since --- the incident. He's completely demoralized."

"Never knew dogs were so touchy," Ox said.

"Dogs have feelings just like people," Baughman said, indignantly. "How would you like to be stripped naked for the world to see?"

A mental image flashed through my mind. It wasn't pretty.

"Yeah, I guess," Ox said, apologetically. "How did the perp get into the house?"

"Back door," Baughman said, pointing.

Just like the home of the first invasion, a small window had been broken, allowing access to the deadbolt.

"Any thoughts as to who might have done this?" I asked.

Baughman shook his head. "None! I just can't get my head around why someone would do this. It makes no sense."

I had to agree with him on that.

We called the lab boys, knowing full well that they would come up empty, but we had to try.

We bid farewell to Morton Baughman and as I took one last look into the dog's sad eyes, it actually grieved me to think, after all the years of humming that song, that something could actually stop the Duke of Earl."

Back in the cruiser, Ox's thoughts, as they often do, turned to food.

"So I guess we're taking the girls to dinner tonight. Any idea where?"

"Nope. Maggie told me she'd let me know when I got home."

"Well I hope it's someplace good. Last night, I actually dreamed about a big, juicy T-bone and a loaded baked potato. When I woke up, I'd been drooling on my pillow."

I had heard about 'wet dreams', but this was a new one.

Later that afternoon, when I pulled up in front of the three-story apartment building that I own,

Professor Skinner and Jerry Singer were sitting on the front porch.

Maggie and I occupy the entire third story of this brownstone beast on Armour Boulevard. The other four apartments are occupied by my dad, his octogenarian squeeze, Bernice, the Professor and Jerry. My old friend and maintenance man, Willie, lives in a studio apartment in the basement.

If there ever were another odd couple to compete with Tony Randall and Jack Klugman, it would be Jerry and the Professor. They are as opposite as night and day. The Professor was my mentor during my university days. His studies included philosophy, psychology and sociology. Over the years, his scholarly insights have guided me through some rough and troublesome times. Jerry, on the other hand, lives only to tell jokes, hence the name we have given him, Jerry the Joker. For some reason, the two have bonded, and on rare occasions, the usually somber Professor will actually crack a joke. Unfortunately, we haven't seen any signs that Jerry has picked up any of the Professor's intellectual traits.

Jerry was waving a copy of the *Kansas City Star*. "Walt! You and Ox are in the paper. The Dynamic Duo has made the news!"

I had seen the article about the dog-shaving intruder earlier. I was hoping no one else would notice.

"Why would *ANYONE* break into a house just to shave a dog? That's just crazy!"

Coming from Jerry, that was quite an indictment.

"That's the $64,000 dollar question," I replied. "If we had a motive, we might have somewhere to start."

"I've got a dog joke. You wanna hear it?"

"Do I have a choice?"

"Not really, but I thought I'd ask just to be polite. Anyway, two guys were walking down the street when they came across a dog sitting on the sidewalk studiously licking his balls. 'Oh boy, I'd like to do that,' sighed one man enviously. 'Go right ahead,' encouraged his friend. 'But if I were you, I'd pat him first'."

"Very funny."

Not to be outdone, the Professor weighed in. "A continuation of that very old and tired joke is the question 'why do dogs do it?' and the usual answer is 'because they can', but actually, ball licking may be an indication that the dog has a skin disorder. By the way, did you know that there is archeological proof that dogs were domesticated and have been man's best friend for over 14,000 years?"

This was way more than I wanted to know about canis lupus familiaris. "Thanks for all of that, but Maggie is waiting for me."

As I headed up the stairs, Jerry got off a parting shot. "What do you call a dog with no legs? Doesn't matter. He won't come anyway."

When I opened the door, Maggie was standing there with purse in hand, ready for our evening out.

"What took you so long?"

"I got waylaid by Frick and Frack on the front porch. We'd better leave by the back stairs or we'll never get away."

"So what is our dining destination?" I asked as we made our way across town to pick up Ox and Judy.

"It's a surprise. You'll just have to wait till we're all together to find out."

Her response sent a shiver down my spine. Her 'dining surprises' more often than not, had turned out to be 'dining disasters' to my picky palate.

We had just turned off the expressway, when I noticed a billboard. It read, 'Heart of America Kennel Club Dog Show'. The event was to be held in Bartle Hall in downtown Kansas City. I made a mental note to mention this to Ox.

Once we were all in the car, I inquired, "Okay, where to? What's the big surprise?"

"Head for the Plaza," Maggie replied.

"Our first thought was to eat a JJ's," Judy said.

"JJ's is good," Ox replied. "They have a fantastic Kansas City Strip steak."

"Well, that was our first thought, but then Jane, one of Maggie's friends at the real estate office, told her about the Melting Pot. It sounded fun and different, so that's where we're going."

"What makes it different?" I asked apprehensively.

"It's a fondue restaurant," Maggie replied proudly.

"What's fondue?" Ox asked.

"It's fun!" Judy replied. "You cook your own food right at your table in special little pots of bubbling liquid."

"I'm going out to eat and I have to cook my own dinner?" Ox asked incredulously.

"Don't be a big poop," Judy scolded. "You'll love it."

"So we're doing this because of your friend, Jane Fondue?" I quipped.

Maggie punched me in the arm.

We pulled into the covered parking garage and immediately, the smell of sizzling steaks from JJ's just around the corner filled our nostrils.

"Not too late to change," Ox said, hopefully.

"Suck it up, big guy," Judy replied. "This is 'ladies night out', so it's fondue for you."

"Swell!"

When we were seated, the server, a perky little gal with a ponytail, brought the menu with the wine list. I knew we were in trouble right away. There were fifty different kinds of wine, but no Arbor Mist.

"Have you dined with us before?" she asked cheerfully.

"Nope, first time," I replied.

"Then I'd like to recommend our Four Course Experience. It includes a cheese fondue, a salad, an entree and a chocolate fondue for dessert. How does that sound?"

Maggie and Judy were delighted. Ox and I shrugged and nodded. When in Rome --- !

I looked at the cheese choices. I knew about cheddar. Mel puts that on just about everything he has on the menu. I had never heard of Emmenthaler Swiss. I'm always dubious about things I can't pronounce.

The cheese arrived bubbling in a pot and we were presented with tiny little forks and a plate of stuff that we were to dip in the pot of cheese.

"Isn't this fun!" Maggie gushed as she and Judy jumped into dipping mode.

I reluctantly had to admit that it tasted pretty good.

Salads came next and then the entree.

Our plates were divided into sections like the plastic plate that mom always had for me because I didn't like the various food groups on my plate to touch each other.

Another bubbling pot of liquid that I learned was 'Seasoned Court Bouillon' appeared. It was in this bubbling cauldron that we were to cook our evening meal.

I could see that Ox was struggling as he speared the teeny-weeny piece of steak with the itsy-bitsy fork and plop it in the pot. I had seen my friend wolf down a 24-ounce Porterhouse in less time than it took to cook his first little tidbit. There was no doubt in my mind that Ox would be going home hungry.

The highlight of my fondue experience was the dessert. Fresh strawberries, bananas, cheesecake, marshmallows and bits of brownies were available to dip in a pot of warm, rich, creamy milk chocolate.

When it was all over and done, I concluded that the meal was not about the destination, but the journey.

Maggie and Judy were deliriously happy, which was a good thing, because when mama's happy, everyone's happy. Well, maybe not Ox.

At the very least, we had discharged our husbandly duty to treat our ladies to a girl's night out. Next time, Ox and I would get to choose.

We were ambling back to the parking garage, when an explosion that dwarfed anything I had ever experienced, shook the ground.

Windows shattered in the multi-storied office building across the street. We ducked into the garage as glass rained down onto the street.

When the shock from the initial blast had subsided we hurried around the corner and were horrified to see that all that remained of JJ's restaurant was a piece of the front facade. What had been the interior of the restaurant was engulfed in flames.

People were sitting and laying in the street in shock and we could see others stumbling from the burning inferno and collapsing, gasping for breath.

As we approached, a fireman held up his hand. "Please, stay back."

Ox showed the fireman his badge. "Three of us are off duty cops. How can we help?"

"Thank God," he replied. "Help us keep people away from the scene until the first responders arrive. They should be here any minute."

We heard sirens blaring in the distance.

"Any idea what happened?" I asked.

"Looks like some construction guys were digging a trench and hit a gas line. The restaurant filled with gas and ignited. That's about all we know right now."

For the next three hours, we helped where we could while the firemen battled the raging blaze and ambulances carried the injured to area hospitals.

At midnight, with our clothing smelling of smoke and our faces smudged with ash, we headed back to our car. It would be hours, maybe days before the full impact of the tragedy would be known.

I took one last look at the once-elegant restaurant that had been serving its patrons for almost thirty years, and I reflected on our conversation when we had parked earlier in the evening.

Had our ladies not insisted that we try something new, we might have been among those staggering from the burning building --- or worse.

I made a mental note to thank Jane for telling Maggie about the Melting Pot. She may have just saved our lives.

CHAPTER 6

Henry Martin spent a restless night. He tossed and turned and when he did manage to drift into fitful slumber, his dreams were filled with horrifying images of being relentlessly pursued by sinister figures.

Before tumbling wearily into bed, he had tried to picture himself pulling the trigger and firing the bullet that would kill the President of the United States, but the scenario was so far removed from his frame of reference, he simply couldn't realistically imagine himself committing such an atrocity.

Henry wasn't unfamiliar with guns. As a youth, he had hunted small game with his dad, but that was twenty years ago. There were no guns in his home and he couldn't remember the last time he had actually held one.

After the phone conversation with the mysterious stranger, he had wadded up the paper with the call-back number and tossed it in the trash, but when he returned to the basement to sort through the next box of memorabilia that had to be sorted and disposed of, he returned to the kitchen and salvaged the discarded number.

In those rare moments when he actually contemplated pulling the trigger, his thoughts focused on the consequences to himself and to his family.

He knew that he could be shot right on the spot by the Secret Service and at the very least, he would spend the rest of his life in prison. After a great deal of thought, he realized that he was willing to sacrifice himself for the good of his family, but what about his family? Even though they would be set financially, they would forever live with the stigma of being related to an assassin.

Maybe that wasn't so bad. Who remembers or ever even knew the families of Lee Harvey Oswald or Sirhan Sirhan.

It surprised him that he was actually considering the consequences of accepting the mysterious man's proposal.

He had pretty much put the matter out of his head when he heard the mailman at the door.

Among the solicitations and ads was a letter from Acme Collections. Mastercard had turned his account over to the agency to hound him for payment. He had expected that one.

The other letter was from his insurance company. His grace period had expired. His family -- - his wife and child, had no medical insurance.

He fell into a chair and wept. Everything that he had worked for, for twelve long years, was gone -- - wiped away, and his family would soon be wards of the state.

When his sobbing had subsided, he pulled the crinkled scrap of paper from his pocket. He stared at it for the longest time and finally picked up the phone and dialed.

"Henry," said the electronically altered voice, "I was hoping I would hear from you."

"Listen, I'm not making any commitment ---

not yet anyway. I just have some questions. How exactly would this work?"

"It's really very simple. We will need you for about a week to sharpen your skills with a firearm. The president will be coming to Kansas City to cut the ribbon on a new preschool for inner city kids. You will be standing close by for the event. When the time is right, you'll do your thing. Don't worry. We'll coach you every step of the way."

"What will happen after the president goes down?"

"If you do exactly as we say, you will be fine. You will immediately lay your weapon on the ground, fall to your knees and raise your arms. With all the press around, all they can do is arrest you and take you into custody. You'll be a model prisoner."

"What about the money?"

"What about it?"

"The only way I could be sure that Marsha has the money is if it's wired to an offshore account in her name and I verify the deposit before I pull the trigger."

"I see that you've given this some thought. Of course we would agree to those conditions. We want this to be a win-win situation."

"Let me think about this some more. I'll be in touch."

Henry disconnected and stood motionless. *"Am I actually considering this?"* he wondered.

After squad meeting the next morning, I pulled Ox aside.

"With all the excitement from the explosion, I forgot to mention something I saw."

"What's that, partner?"

"A billboard. It was advertising a dog show sponsored by the Heart of America Kennel Club. It got me thinking about those three fancy dogs. If they were planning to compete in the show, that might be the link that we've been missing."

"It's worth a shot," he replied. "Let's make some calls."

I found Mrs. Fitzhugh's number in my notebook and dialed her number.

"Mrs. Fitzhugh, this is Officer Williams. We were at your home a few days ago. I have a follow-up question for you."

"Certainly, Officer. How can I help?"

"Were you planning on entering Lazzie in the Heart of America Kennel Club dog show?"

"I was, but I obviously can't now. We're very disappointed."

"Is it possible that your dog was shaved to remove you from the competition?"

"Well, I suppose that's possible, but I can't imagine anyone going to all that trouble considering what's to be gained."

"And what would that be?"

"The winners will receive trophies, of course, and the recognition that goes with being declared a winner, but that's the same as it's always been. The competition has always been spirited, but never mean and vicious."

"Thank you, Mrs. Fitzhugh. You've been a big help."

"What do you think?" I asked, after hanging up.

"I think it's worth two more calls."

Calls to Morton Baughman and Edith Barksdale were much the same. Both had planned to enter the dog show, but had abandoned the idea after the shaving.

"Time for a conference with the Captain," Ox said.

It was a weary Captain that greeted us. He had been summoned after the explosion on the Plaza and hadn't yet been home to sleep.

"What's up, guys?"

"We may have found a connection between the three dog shaving incidents. It's pretty thin, but it's all we've got."

"Let's hear it."

The Captain listened quietly as we related our calls to the three victims.

"We thought it would be worth a conversation with the dog show promoters to see if there was something special about this event that would encourage someone to eliminate the competition," I concluded.

"Do it," the Captain replied. "I want to get this thing wrapped up. We have bigger fish to fry. I know this is important to those three owners, but there are actually murders, rapes and muggings that need our attention. By the way, thank you both, and Judy, for your help last night. Keeping the crowd back gave the first responders room to do their jobs."

"We just wish we could have done more," Ox replied. "Any report on the casualties yet?"

"One death and fifteen injured, some critically. A real tragedy."

"Sorry to hear that. Let us know if we can help --- even off duty."

"Thanks, Ox. I'll keep that in mind. Right now, just get that damn dog shaver off the street."

A visit to the website of the Kennel Club led us to the show chairman, Richard Reese, who agreed to meet with us later that morning.

"How can we be of help to the Police Department?" Reese asked, offering us a chair in his office. "This is my secretary, Miss Biggs. Can she get you anything?"

"No, we're fine," I replied. "This may just be a shot in the dark. Have you read in the paper about the home invasions where the dogs were shaved?"

"I have," he replied, shaking his head.

"Unconscionable! Why would anyone do such a horrible thing?"

"We were hoping you could tell us," Ox replied. "All three of the dogs were going to be in the show, but have cancelled because of the shaving. Is there anything special or different about this show that would make someone want to eliminate the competition?"

Reese and Miss Biggs exchanged worried looks.

"I'm guessing that there is," Ox observed. "Anything you'd like to share with us?"

"Well, there is," he replied, reluctantly, "but it's been a closely guarded secret. Only a handful of people knew about it."

"Go on," Ox encouraged.

"Maurice, The Wonder Dog!"

"Excuse, me?"

"It's a new sitcom on one of the major TV networks. The production company has sent a team of observers to dog shows all over the country. They're looking for the next big dog star --- the next Lassie or Rin Tin Tin. They've kept the whole thing under wraps. If word got out, the owners of every mutt in the state would flood the shows. It would be a three ring circus."

"Obviously someone out there knows," I said, "and they've been eliminating the competition. I'm afraid you have a leak in your organization. You said only a handful of people knew. We're going to need a list."

"Of course. The last thing we want is for our club to be responsible for this kind of behavior. You will have our full cooperation."

The Captain was just heading out the door to go home and get some shut-eye.

"Anything substantial?"

I nodded. "I think we've found our motive."

For the second time that morning, the Captain sat quietly while we shared the information we had gleaned from Richard Reese.

"Maurice the Wonder Dog! Just what the world needs. Another dumb TV show."

"I would agree," Ox replied, "but whoever owns the dog selected for the part will become very wealthy overnight. People have murdered, not just shaved, for a lot less than that."

"You're right, of course. We need to get a handle on this thing before it escalates into something more drastic. You said that the kennel club would cooperate. What about the network?"

"Reese thought that they would be supportive," I replied. "The last thing they want is for their new sitcom to start out with a scandal."

"Good!" the Captain said with a smile. "Walt, it looks like you're going undercover."

"What! Why me?"

"Because you're our undercover guy, that's

why. You've got more experience than anyone else in the squad and you just look like a network executive --- well, you will after you get a haircut. Have Maggie trim your ear and nose hairs too. As soon as the word gets around that you're part of the team judging the dogs, there's no question that our perp will try to influence you."

"But I don't even like dogs!"

"You do now!"

CHAPTER 7

I'm not a dog person --- at least not right now.

It's not that I don't like dogs; it's just that it's so difficult to own one in an apartment in the city while working a full time job.

One of my fondest memories is of my grandfather's old dog, Scrappy. As a kid, when I visited the farm, which was almost every weekend, old Scrappy was right there to greet me, wagging his tail in anticipation. The two of us spent treasured hours hunting small game in the forests and fields surrounding the farm.

I don't ever remember Scrappy setting foot in the house, but he was always there by the back door to tag along when Grandpa and I did our chores. He was always on guard to keep the foxes away from the chicken house and the coons out of the trash.

Over fifty years later, I still vividly remember the day when Scrappy, old, weary and barely able to move, left us. Grandpa took Scrappy and his rifle out behind the barn. "Time to put him down," Grandpa said. "It's the right thing to do."

I cried for days.

I love Elvis songs, but to this day, I cannot listen to his soulful rendition of *Old Shep* without tears running down my cheeks.

> *As the years fast did roll, Old Shep*
> *he grew old*
> *His eyes were fast growing dim.*

And one day the doctor looked at me and said
I can't do no more for him, Jim.

During those years when I was living alone, before Maggie came into my life, I thought about getting a canine companion, but then I would look out the window on a cold winter morning and see Mrs. Bigelow from next door, shivering in the cold while her little mutt was trying to squeeze one out. After he had finished his business, she would dutifully bend down and scoop up the steamy deposit in a plastic bag.

I didn't need that.

I would go to someone's home and watch as their dog scooted his rear end across the carpet. I had heard that was a sign of worms, or maybe his butt just itched. Either way, I didn't want that on my carpet.

Then there's the drool. I just don't do drool, so, no dog for me in the city.

Per the Captain's request, I got a haircut and trimmed the offending follicles from my ears and nose with my Remington Turbo. I put on my best suit and headed downtown to Bartle Hall.

The actual representative from the TV network was a perky little gal named Mandy. For the purposes of our undercover operation, she would tag along as my administrative assistant, but would still be doing the evaluations.

Ox would be roaming the halls as a custodian, keeping things neat and tidy for the entrants and the spectators.

Richard Reese and his assistant, Miss Biggs, met with Ox, Mandy and me before the show started to finalize our plan.

It really wasn't much of a plan. Our hypothesis was that one of the entrants had gotten the information about the TV gig from someone on the Kennel Club staff. We were hoping that the perp would approach me as the TV rep, and try to influence me in some way. If no one did, we were back to square one.

Reese had given us a list of Kennel Club members that knew about the TV show, but there was nothing that singled any one of them out as the source of the leak.

We were on the way to our seats when a big Labrador Retriever ambled up and licked me on the hand. When I stopped to pat him on the head, he looked up at me with soft brown eyes that would melt even the coldest heart. He looked just like *Old Yeller* from that 1957 movie classic.

"That's Jimbo," Reese said. "He belongs to Billy, one of our members that has been helping us put on this show for years. Jimbo is kind of our unofficial mascot. He has the run of the place."

I knelt down and rubbed the big dog's ears. He had the kind of face that screamed, "Take me home!"

I wavered momentarily, but then I took another look at his size and figured that it would take at least a quart sandwich bag to accommodate one of his little gifts.

I gave him a final pat and as I walked away, I felt a gentle nudge on my behind.

"I think he likes you," Reese observed.

This rear-ender was a new experience for me. In my previous encounters with big dogs, they had invariably gone straight for Mr. Winkie and the boys.

As we walked through the back halls of the arena, there were dogs and owners of every description.

Somewhere out there was an owner that would stoop to dirty tricks to secure the coveted TV spot.

But which one?

Henry Martin sat in the car outside his in-laws home for a long time.

This was his first visit since Marsha and Billy had moved in with her parents and he wasn't sure how he would be received.

Jim and Ellen Bennett had always been friendly and supportive, but Marsha was their baby girl and nothing was too good for her.

Jim was a hard-nosed old cuss that took the role of alpha-male and family provider seriously. He had been in the military and served two terms in Vietnam.

Realizing that he couldn't avoid the inevitable, Henry climbed out of the car and knocked on the door.

When Marsha opened the door, Billy threw his arms around him.

"I missed you, Dad."

"I missed you too, Son."

Marsha pried the boy away and gave Henry a kiss and a hug.

"Come on in, sweetie. Mom has dinner ready."

Ellen set a heaping plate of fried chicken on the table and gave Henry a peck on the cheek. "Hope you're hungry. I made all your favorites."

"Thanks, Mom. You didn't have to go to all this trouble."

"Nonsense! Jim has been bugging me for fried chicken for a week."

Jim Bennett grabbed Henry's arm and shook his hand. "Have a seat, son, and tell us what's going on."

Jim was never one to mince words.

"Plenty of time for that later," Ellen said. "Let's eat."

Henry tried his best to eat enthusiastically for Ellen's benefit, but the knot in his stomach made it nearly impossible.

After Billy helped his grandmother clear the table, Jim said, "Billy, why don't you go play your video game so that we grownups can have a talk?"

"But Grandpa," he protested, "I want to hear what's going on too."

"Not this time. You run along now."

After Billy had stalked off, Jim turned to his son-in-law. "So what's happening, Henry? Any luck finding a job?"

Henry hung his head. "Nothing yet. The companies aren't hiring for the jobs I'm qualified for and I can't even get hired to flip burgers. They say I'm overqualified with my MBA. They don't want to hire and train someone that they know will be moving on sooner or later."

Jim shook his head disgustedly. "It's not your fault, son. You couldn't help it when they shipped your job off to Mexico. It's those damned politicians!

"There's just no middle class anymore. At one end, you've got the fat cats --- the rich getting richer, and at the other end, you've got the people living on the public dole. Guys like us; we just don't stand a chance. They make it impossible for the small businessman to survive, so they move somewhere else, and now the president wants to legalize eleven million more foreigners to take our jobs. It just isn't right!"

"I appreciate you saying that, Jim, and you have no idea how much I appreciate you letting Marsha and Billy stay here until we can get back on our feet."

"Glad to help. That's what families do. I wish we could help more. The three of you are welcome here as long as need be, but, well, there's just not much we can do for you financially. Ellen and I are on a fixed income now. Got a whopping twenty-dollar a month increase in Social Security this year. Paid into that damn thing for forty years and we barely have enough to get by on."

"I know, Jim. We wouldn't think about asking you for money. Something will turn up. I know it will."

"I have faith in you. You're a hard worker --- always done what had to be done to take care of your family. I know you will again."

Henry could think of only one thing that could pull his family out of the hole they were in. He wondered what Jim Bennett would think about that.

After a dessert of apple cobbler, he rose from the table.

"I'd better get back. Those things aren't going to pack themselves."

"Awww, Dad! Do you have to leave so soon?" Billy wailed.

"Don't want to, but I have to. You be good and take care of you mother for me. Can I count on you?"

"Sure!"

"That's my boy."

At the front door, Marsha pulled Henry close.

"You know that I'm with you and I'll always love you."

"No matter what?" he asked, thinking about the mysterious man's proposition.

"No matter what!"

CHAPTER 8

The first hour just seemed like an hour, but the second hour seemed like two hours and the third hour seemed like a whole day. Wait! That's a line from the Steve Martin movie, *The Jerk*, but that's exactly how I felt after watching dozens of dogs cavorting around the arena, most ignoring their master's coaching.

When the lunch break finally rolled around, I headed to the nearest concession stand.

Ox was in line just ahead of me.

"What's up, partner?" he asked.

"I'm gonna get a dog," I replied.

"Whoa! Really? I thought you were opposed to dogs in your apartment."

"A HOT DOG! But you knew that. I'm starving. How was your morning?"

"You wouldn't believe how many piles of poop I've cleaned up and how many times I've heard, 'Oh, my goodness! FiFi has never done that before.'"

"Are you taking names? Maybe you can go take a dump in their front yard to get even."

"Very funny!"

At that moment I felt a cold nose rub against my hand. It was Jimbo.

"I think you've found a friend," Ox observed.

I reached down to pet him and got a handful of drool for my trouble.

"Great! Now I'll have to go wash up from one dog before I can tackle the dog I've been waiting for all morning."

Just then, the intercom blared, "George Wilson. Clean up behind Section 27."

Ox heaved a sigh, "That's me. Doody calls!"

Ox headed off with his pooper-scooper and I headed to the washroom with Jimbo dutifully tagging along behind.

I had finished washing up and had stopped by the water fountain before returning to the concession stand.

I felt something soft and warm snuggling up to my backside and wondered what Jimbo was up to now.

When I turned, it wasn't Jimbo, but a gorgeous brunette that had invaded my personal space.

"Oh, sorry!" I said, trying to back away, but there was nowhere to go.

"Don't be sorry," she purred, pressing even closer. "My name is Michelle. How was your morning?"

"Uhhhh, just fine," I stammered. "Were you wanting to use the fountain?"

I tried slipping to the side, but she blocked me with a curvaceous leg and pressed even closer.

"Not really," she replied, as she nuzzled my chest with her ample bosom. "I've been watching you all morning and I thought maybe we could take a little break together."

After my initial shock had worn off, it dawned on me that it probably wasn't my animal magnetism that had drawn this vixen to me, but the fact that I was from the TV production company. This gal was undoubtedly part of the shaving crew. I knew I had to play along.

"What exactly did you have in mind?" I asked in my huskiest voice.

"I know a little room that's very private. It has no windows and it locks. We could get to know one another better."

"Lead on," I said, taking her hand.

She led me to a room that was exactly as she had described. After locking the door, she pointed to a comfy couch. "Let's get down to business."

She smiled and gave me a wink as she started unbuttoning her blouse.

As the buttons popped open, I figured it was time to switch gears before things got out of hand. I had always shared my undercover adventures with Maggie. Up to this time, she had been very supportive, even when I ended up shot or beaten, but I didn't think what was about to happen would go over very well.

"Look," I said, "I --- uhhh --- appreciate your --- uhhh --- enthusiasm, but let's get real. A gal like you just doesn't get all hot and bothered by an old fart like me. What's really going on here?"

"Besides," I said, pointing to my wedding ring, "I'm happily married. So what gives?"

I saw the disgusted look on her face as she quickly re-buttoned her blouse.

"Okay, so you're too old to be interested in

the temptations of the flesh ---."

"Hold on a minute," I protested, "I didn't say that I couldn't. I said that I wouldn't. There's a big difference."

"Whatever," she replied, waving her hand. "Let's cut to the chase. We both know that you're with the TV production company checking out the dogs for the *Maurice, The Wonder Dog Show*. We want that spot. What's it going to take? Money? I can give you five thousand right now!"

I figured that it was time to go for the confession.

"I'll bet that you want that spot so bad, you'd even shave a few competitor's dogs to get it."

That caught her by surprise. For a brief moment, she was speechless, and then I saw the light bulb go off in her eyes.

"You're a cop, aren't you? A damned cop!"

I pulled my badge from my pocket. "Got me!"

"Well I have a little surprise for you," she said, heisting up her skirt.

Strapped to her thigh was a holster holding a snub-nosed .38.

I couldn't help but wonder how she would have explained that if our aborted tryst had progressed any farther.

"Sorry, old timer, but now that we know where we both stand, I can't let you waltz out of here and blow this whole thing for us."

"A .38 makes a pretty loud pop," I said. "That's going to be pretty hard to explain to all of the folks roaming the hall just outside the door."

"You're right, of course, but I have a better idea. Go where I tell you and no one else will get hurt. If you screw this up, a whole lot more people will wind up with a bullet."

For the second time in an hour, I told the gorgeous brunette to lead on.

"Head down the hall and take the first right turn --- and no tricks!"

The first right turn led us into a small banquet room that was unoccupied during the dog show.

"Through that door," she said, pushing me with the muzzle of the .38.

The door led into a fully stocked kitchen. At the far end was the door to a walk-in freezer.

"Open it!" she ordered.

I opened the door and a cloud of smoky haze billowed forth as the frigid air in the freezer mingled with the warm humid air in the kitchen.

She gave me a shove and I stumbled in. Before the door slammed shut behind me, I saw a side of beef hanging from a hook and boxes of frozen vegetables.

I heard her muffled voice through the door. "You should have taken me up on the sex. It would have been a lot more fun than this."

I was beginning to think she was right. My frozen body was going to be harder to explain to Maggie than a roll in the hay with a gorgeous stranger. Well, maybe not.

It was pitch black and I could feel the icy cold

71

sapping the strength from my body.

I had read about pilots that had been downed in icy seawater. The article said that a person could last for up to an hour in 40-degree water before hypothermia renders them unconscious.

I had never read how long a person could survive in a sub-zero freezer.

I was about to find out.

Ox had finally gotten his foot long hot dog with chili and cheese when Mandy approached him.

"Hi Ox. Have you seen Walt?

Ox looked at his watch. "Not for about a half hour. He was headed to the wash room, then he was going to come back here for a bite of lunch."

Ox turned to the kid behind the counter. "Have you seen the old dude that I was talking to a half hour ago?"

"Nope, he never came back. Maybe he got a dog from another concession stand."

"Yeah, maybe," Ox said, never believing a word of it. "Let's check out the men's room. Maybe he got sick."

Ox checked every stall, but there was no sign of his friend.

"It's just not like him to disappear like this."

At that moment, Jimbo appeared. He sat at Ox's feet and whimpered.

"You again. If you hadn't drooled on Walt's hand, we probably wouldn't be looking for him now."

At first, Jimbo looked hurt, but then he got to his feet, grabbed Ox's trouser leg in his big jaws and pulled.

"Get away from me, Mutt. I don't have time to play now. My partner is missing."

"I don't think he's playing," Mandy said. "I know dogs and this one is trying to tell us something. What is it, Jimbo? Where's Walt?"

The big dog ran a few feet and turned around expectantly.

"He wants us to follow him," Mandy said.

"You can tell by that?"

"Trust me!"

Jimbo ran a few feet more. When he saw that he was being followed, he took off at a dead run.

"Hey, slow down!" Ox yelled. "I only have two legs. You have four."

They followed Jimbo down the hall, through the banquet room and into the kitchen.

He squatted in front of the big freezer and pawed the door as if he was digging a hole.

"It's locked!" Mandy cried.

Ox looked around the kitchen and spotted a huge meat cleaver.

"Stand back," he ordered.

It took only two blows for the lock to spring open.

Ox threw open the door and his partner rolled

out onto the floor curled up in a fetal position.

"Jesus, Walt! Are you okay?"

"What took you so long?" came the feeble reply.

"Had to finish my chili dog," the big guy replied with relief.

"How --- how did you find me?"

Jimbo ambled up and gave Walt a big lick on the face leaving a stream of drool.

"Thank your furry friend here. If he hadn't come along, you would be a sixty-nine-year-old popsicle."

"You know what," Mandy said. "I think we might have just found Maurice, The Wonder Dog!"

CHAPTER 9

The silence was oppressive as Henry Martin opened the door into his dark, lonely house.

He could *almost* hear Billy's voice as he would come running from his playroom. "Mom! Daddy's home!" --- Almost.

He could *almost* smell the fragrant aroma of apple pie coming from the kitchen, baked by the loving hands of his wife. --- Almost.

Tonight there was nothing but emptiness.

The life and love had been sucked from his home by the terrible burden of debt and despair.

He switched on the floor lamp and sunk into the recliner where he had watched movies and sports on cable TV --- back in the happier days when they had cable. It had been turned off months ago.

Billy's Tonka dump truck that he had carried from the playroom to be boxed up for a garage sale sat in the corner. Billy had spent hours in the sandbox in the backyard with that truck. There was plenty of room in the basement to keep this treasured toy, but no room at Jim and Ellen's. The truck would have to go.

He remembered his father-in-law's words earlier in the day. "I have faith in you. You're a hard worker --- always done what had to be done to take care of your family. I know you will again."

He knew the answer to his family's dilemma all too well.

He wondered what Jim would think if he

actually carried it out. Would he be proud that he had taken care of his family or ashamed that Henry was part of the family?

He remembered Marsha's words as she held him close. "You know that I'm with you and I'll always love you, no matter what."

But would she still love him when she learned that he had taken the life of the highest elected official in the land?

He sat pondering those questions when the light flickered, then went out. KCP&L had made good on their promise to disconnect service if the bill was not paid.

He sat in the darkness for the longest time, feeling the temperature in the house drop ever so slowly.

Finally, with a resolve born of despair, he pulled the crumpled slip of paper from his pocket.

The only light in the cold dark room came from his cell phone as he dialed the number.

"I'm in!"

It took a half hour wrapped in blankets and two cups of steaming coffee to thaw me out.

The moment I was able to speak, I told Ox about my encounter with the dog show Mata Hari. It didn't take him long to find her. She was, by far, the best-looking handler in the show.

Later, after he had heard the whole story, he just shook his head. "So you took a pass on that?"

"And you wouldn't have? Have you considered the consequences if Judy found out?"

"Most likely she would have broken both my legs and cracked my skull after rendering my private parts inoperable. In retrospect, I think you made the right call."

"Any word on her accomplice?"

"With the charge of attempted murder of a police officer hanging over her head, she sang like a canary. Turns out that she and one of the guys on Reese's staff were old high school sweethearts. They hooked up again at a class reunion and hatched the plot."

That brought a smile to my face. I had just experienced my own class reunion and I was well aware of the shenanigans that could resurface as old acquaintances and friends reunited.

By the time we returned to the precinct, the news that we had collared the dog-shaving ring had spread throughout the squad.

Officer Dooley was the first to get in his licks. "Hey, it's the Ice Man and the Dog Whisperer. I hear you were a really cool guy --- I mean REALLY COOL!"

"Very funny!"

Fortunately, the Captain called us into his office before anyone could launch a second volley.

"Great job, guys. I'm so happy that we can finally put this dog-shaving thing to bed. Take the rest of the day off."

Then with a straight face, he handed me an envelope. "In recognition of your brush with death, your fellow officers took up a collection and bought you this."

I opened the envelope and found a gift certificate for an hour under the lamp in a tanning booth.

"They thought it might help you thaw out," he said, trying to suppress a smile.

"Et tu, Brute?" I said, with as much angst as I could muster.

"Too good to pass up," he said with a grin. "Now get out of here!"

When I pulled up in front of my apartment building, my old friend and maintenance man, Willie Duncan was sitting on the front step.

At one point in my life, I had owned two hundred rental units. Willie was the guy I counted on to take care of all the clogged toilets, broken windows and drippy faucets.

When I retired from real estate I sold all of my buildings except the one I live in and the Three Trails Hotel, a flophouse with twenty sleeping rooms that share four hall baths. No one in their right mind wanted to buy that old relic.

Willie lives in a studio apartment in the basement and gets his rent-free for taking care of the last vestiges of my rental empire.

Since becoming a cop, Willie has proven to be a valuable asset. Before starting to work for me, he lived on the street in the seamier parts of Kansas City, and that background has helped solve more than one case. My old friend had pulled my fat out of the fire more times than I wanted to remember.

"Hey, Mr. Walt. You home early."

"Ox and I wrapped up a case and the Captain gave us the rest of the day off. How are things around here?"

"Dey's quiet for a change. I seen Jerry head off somewhere, so I don' have to lissen to none of his stupid jokes, an yo' dad an' Miss Bernice went to de movies."

"Fantastic! I've had a rather trying day, so I'm about to pour a glass of Arbor Mist and just kick back for a while."

"Sounds good to me. Enjoy yousef."

At that moment, the phone rang.

"Walt, this is Mary. Some punks just drove by and shot up the hotel!"

So much for taking it easy.

Willie saw the look of concern on my face. "Whassup?"

"That was Mary. She said there had been a drive-by shooting at the hotel. Let's go!"

Mary Murphy is my seventy-six year old housemother at the hotel. Given the fact that virtually all of the tenants there are either old retired guys on Social Security or marginally employable fellows working out of the day labor pool, somebody had to be on site to keep a lid on things. That person is Mary.

While most old gals in their seventies are not exactly formidable, Mary is definitely an exception.

In the past three years, she has clubbed an assassin that had Maggie and me in his sights, shot an intruder that had threatened her with a knife and whacked the intruder's brother that had come looking for revenge. She carries a thirty-six inch baseball bat and no one at the hotel gives her a minute of trouble.

When I pulled up in front of the hotel, a black and white was already there. The officer recognized me right away.

"Walt, what are you doing here?"

"Unfortunately, I own the place. What have you got?"

"I'll tell you what we got!" Mary shouted from the front porch. "We got bullet holes and lots of 'em."

I looked where she was pointing and at least a dozen bullets had shattered the old asbestos tile on the front of the building.

"Was anyone hurt?"

"Nope, no one got shot, but old man Feeney

was sittin' on the far end of the porch when the shootin' started. Scared him so bad, he crapped his pants. He peeled 'em off and was headed to the laundry room but I stopped him. I told him no way was he gonna put those nasty things in my machine."

That was way more information than I wanted.

Mary forged ahead. "I think they was shootin' at that kid," she said, pointing to a young black man sitting on the stoop.

"Darius!" Willie exclaimed. "You all right, boy?"

The kid, obviously scared to death, nodded his head.

"Do you know this boy?" the officer asked.

"Sho do," Willie replied. "Dat's Darius. He's Emma's gran'son. I helped him get a room here."

Sixty-nine-year-old Willie had never been married --- at least that I knew of, but he certainly hadn't been shy with women over the years. In fact, he had quite a reputation as a lady's man in his younger days. He had mellowed with age, but he most assuredly hadn't been put out to pasture. On those frequent occasions when he felt the need for a booty call, Emma had been his go-to gal.

"You know who done dis?" Willie asked

The boy nodded again.

"Well who den?"

"The Vipers."

"Holy crap!" the officer said. "I wouldn't want to be in your shoes!"

"So who are these guys?" I asked. I had never heard of the Vipers before.

"They're a new gang. After you and Ox took out the Niners, there was a vacuum, and as the old saying goes, 'nature abhors a vacuum'. It wasn't long before the Vipers started running the streets. From what I've heard from the guys in the Gang Unit, they're every bit as bad, if not worse, than the Niners."

Just what I needed --- straight from the freezer and into the fire --- all in the same day!

CHAPTER 10

Brant Jaeger was ecstatic when he heard Henry's voice on the other line. He covered the mouthpiece and turned to Terrance Cobb. "He's in! He's gonna do it! I knew he would!"

Regaining his composure, he turned his attention back to Henry. "I'm glad to hear it, Henry. Here's what we need to do first ---."

Before he could finish the sentence, Henry broke in. "No, Max, or whatever your name is, if I'm going to put my life on the line, I have a few stipulations of my own."

Henry's boldness took Jaeger by surprise. He had figured him to be weak and submissive. "Very well. What do you have in mind?"

"Money! I'm sitting here in the dark. KCP&L has cut off my electricity. The gas and water are probably not far behind. My home is in foreclosure. If I don't catch up the back payments it will soon be gone. When I go through with this, my days with my wife and child are numbered. I want them to be as pleasant and normal as possible."

Jaeger liked the fact that Henry said, 'when' and not 'if'.

"How much are we talking about?"

"Fifty thousand. I'll set up the bank account tomorrow and text you the account number. When I see the money is there, I'll give you a call. I'll need a few days to get the lights back on and get the wolf away from the door. After that, I'm all yours."

There was a long pause.

"That's doable, Henry. I'm only going to say this once, so listen very carefully. I told you in the beginning that this was a win-win situation. When we pull this off, your family will be set for life and my organization will have accomplished its objective --- but, if at any juncture, you cross us, it will no longer be a win for your family. We know who and where they are, Marsha, Billy, Ellen and Jim. If we are willing to take down the President of the United States, do you think we would hesitate for a minute to take reprisals against your family? Do you understand what I'm saying?"

"Yes, I understand completely. You do what you're supposed to do and I'll do the same."

"I'm glad we're on the same page. I'll be waiting to hear from you. The money will be available to you within an hour from the time we receive your call."

Henry signed off and sat in the darkness pondering the chain of events that he had just set in motion. He had just changed the course of history. The name Henry Martin would be reviled and despised and he would join the ranks of John Wilkes Booth and Lee Harvey Oswald as a murderer of the worst kind.

He allowed himself only a moment to dwell on the dark side of his deed. He focused instead on the salvation of his family.

For the rest of the evening, by the light of a few candles he found in the pantry and the flashlight that he and Billy took fishing, he carried the boxes that he had packed back to the basement and placed them on the wooden shelves where they belonged.

Billy's Tonka truck had been spared the indignity of a garage sale and would be kept in the family so that Billy might some day share it with a son of his own.

He had thought that he would feel remorse and regret for his decision, but instead, he felt a deep sense of relief and satisfaction.

He had saved his family and his home.

After the officer had taken his report and moved on, we had a conference in Mary's apartment.

"Okay, Darius," I said, "tell us what you know about the Vipers."

We had never met before and the young man looked at me skeptically.

Willie stepped right in. "Darius, dis is Mr. Walt. He's my frien' and he's a cop, too. He can help us wit dis. Now tell de man what you know."

I could see that Darius was still reluctant, but with Willie's encouragement, he opened up.

"The dude that's headin' up the Vipers is Rashon Rippe. I knew him from high school before he dropped out. Ever since he started putting the Vipers together, he's been bugging me to join up. I told him that I didn't want no part of it. I'm in Junior

College trying to get my Associate's Degree. He just won't leave me alone."

"There are hundreds of kids out there on the street," I said. "Why is he so interested in you?"

"I tell you why," Willie broke in. "Cuz his pappy was a locksmith and he taught Darius de tricks o' de trade. Dat boy can pop open mos' any lock befo' you can say 'scat'."

"I can certainly see how that could be an asset to a street gang," I replied. "The good news is that this shooting spree was just a message to let Darius know what could happen if he doesn't come around. From the looks of those bullet holes, if they wanted him dead, he'd be dead, but he's no good to them dead. They want his skills."

"Do you think they'll come back?" Darius asked.

Mary had been silent up till now. "I hope they do come back! Mr. Walt, give me a gun and I'll take care of those little punks!"

"I'm sure you could, Mary," I replied, trying to calm her down. "The last thing we need is a shootout at the Three Trails Hotel. I'm concerned about the collateral damage. Right now, all we have is some broken tiles and Mr. Feeney's soiled pants, but it could have been a lot worse. We have to think about the safety of the other nineteen tenants"

"Yeah, I guess you're right," she replied reluctantly, "but I'm keeping' my eyes peeled just the same."

"Did anyone see the driver and the shooter?" I

asked.

"Sorry," Darius replied. "As soon as I saw that souped-up Charger come barreling down the street, I ducked for cover."

"Old man Feeney can't see past the end of the porch," Mary declared, so I know he couldn't tell you nothing'."

"Darius," I said, "I think you should just lay low until we figure this thing out. Go to your classes but keep a low profile. I'm going to check some things out and get back to you."

"What about all them holes in my front porch?" Mary asked.

"Just tell the other tenants that this incident was a warning to one of the tenants that was late with his rent. Maybe they'll get the message."

"I like that!" she said with a grin.

When we were alone. I turned to Willie.

"I think it's time we had a chat with Louie the Lip. Set it up!"

Before Willie came to work for me, he had lived the life of a con man. He and Louie were contemporaries and worked a number of scams as a team. While Willie had given up the life of a grifter, Louie was still out there doing his thing.

They were old friends, and even though their lives had taken different paths, they remained close.

Unlike many of the young punks that roam the streets today, Louie was of the old school. While he lived on the shady side of the law, he still adhered to a moral code. There were just some lines that shouldn't be crossed, no matter what.

Willie had introduced me to Louie and with his help, we had taken some of the more violent and worst offenders off of the street.

Louie came by his moniker honestly. His lower lip stuck out so far, you could almost balance a cup on it. He definitely put Mick Jagger to shame.

Our infrequent conferences with Louie were always hush-hush. He had a reputation to protect and the last thing he wanted was to be seen consorting with a police officer.

We met in an old warehouse on the Northeast side of the city. Willie and Louie did the old hand-slap, knuckle-knock, shoulder bump thing that cool guys do. I could never figure it out. Deferring to my un-coolness, Louie just shook my hand.

"So what can I do for the Bobbsey Twins today?" Louie asked.

"The Vipers," I replied. "What do you know about them?"

"Jesus, Walt! First de Niners and now de Vipers! You got a death wish or somethin'?"

"They're trying to recruit the grandson of Willie's lady friend, and the idiots shot up my hotel this morning. We have to do something."

Louie turned his attention to Willie. "So how is Emma doin' dese days?"

"She's fine! Mighty fine!" Willie replied with a wink.

Apparently Louie and Willie were even closer than I had suspected.

"The Vipers," I repeated, trying to get the conversation back on track. "What makes these guys so tough?"

"They're your typical street gang," Louie replied. "When dey recruit a guy, dey tattoo a snake on his arm, but de snake has no fangs. The member has to earn his fangs by doin' some kind of job. Might be a heist or it might be a killin'. When he pulls it off he gets a fang. The dude's on probation until he gets both of his fangs."

"Well, crap! No wonder the crime rate in Northeast has been on the rise. Where do these guys hang out?"

"Don't know exactly where dey meet to plan their hits, but dey hang out a lot at a place on Twelfth Street. It's a bar with a greasy spoon and some pool tables. Some of em's always there."

"What do you know about this Rashon Rippe? I hear he's running things."

"I suppose you know that I ain't no saint, but I look like Mother Teresa next to this guy. The dude's a regular sociopath. He'd just as soon kill ya as look at ya. I heard dat he gutted one of his own guys for talking back. I'd steer clear of him if I was you."

"Thanks, Louie. You've been a big help. At least I know what I'm dealing with."

"You be careful," he replied. "I went to your funeral once. I don't want to do it again!"

The Captain was surprised to see me back after giving me the day off.

"Just can't stay away, can you?"

"We need to talk."

I told the Captain about Darius, the drive-by shooting at the hotel and our conversation with Louie the Lip.

"How do you get mixed up in all this stuff?" the Captain asked, shaking his head in amazement.

"The Gang Unit has been trying to get a fix on these guys for weeks and here you are, up to your armpits in Vipers. Let's get Franco Harriman over here and see what he has to say.

Harriman was a tough-as-nails veteran that had worked his way up through the ranks and was now the head of the Gang Unit.

In ten minutes, he was in the Captain's office and I got to tell my story for the second time.

He listened intently and I could see by the glimmer in his eyes that he liked what he was hearing.

"This may be the break we've been looking for," he said. "Now I just have to figure how to get some eyes and ears on them without tipping them off."

"I might have an idea," I ventured.

I saw the Captain roll his eyes. "Go on."

"Remember the Gillham Park case with the purse snatcher?"

The Captain nodded.

"Willie and I were staked out in the park --- just two old codgers playing checkers. Nobody pays any attention to old farts like us. We're just part of the woodwork.

"We could set up at the gang's hang out on Twelfth Street. We could just keep our ears and eyes open for a few days. Maybe we could pick up something."

"Why in the world would you want to get involved in this?" Harriman asked. "It's damned dangerous."

"Those punks shot up my hotel today and are trying to recruit a friend of a friend. Someone could have been hurt really bad. I hadn't even heard of these guys until today, but now it's personal."

"Works for me," Harriman said.

The Captain was more reserved. "I don't know, Walt. It's risky business. Promise me that you and Willie will keep a low profile and stay out of trouble."

"I promise."

I had just volunteered to grab a Viper by the tail.

CHAPTER 11

'Max' had been true to his word.

Within an hour of receiving the number for the offshore account, Max had deposited the fifty thousand dollars that Henry had requested.

Henry had spent the day getting the lights back on and paid the other utility bills in person.

He had made a call to the attorney representing his mortgage company and arranged to wire the payments that were in arrears, the accumulated interest and attorney's fees. He was promised that the foreclosure action would be stopped.

As he drove to his in-laws home, he couldn't remember when he had felt so happy. The burden of his family's financial woes had been pressing on him for months and he felt like the weight of the world had been lifted off of his shoulders.

Every so often, the consequences of the price that he would pay for this relief popped into his mind. He pushed the thoughts aside. There would be plenty of time for that later.

As soon as he walked in the door, Marsha could sense that something had changed.

"Henry, something's happened. Tell me!"

Henry knew that this would be coming and he had rehearsed his lines over and over again. He hated that he had to lie, but he couldn't very well tell them that he was being paid to assassinate the president.

Jim and Ellen had heard Marsha's remark and

joined them.

"I have some good news for a change. As you know, I have been submitting my resume for months. It finally paid off. A new IT start-up is opening an office in Kansas City. They said I had all the qualifications they were looking for and hired me on the spot. They even gave me a signing bonus."

"That's fantastic!" Marsha cried, throwing her arms around his neck.

"The only negative," he added, "is that I'll have to be away for about a week. They want me to train in their corporate office."

"What's one more week?" Marsha gushed. "We've been waiting for this break for months."

Jim came up and grabbed Henry's hand. "I'm proud of you, Son. I knew you'd find a way to take care of your family. That's what real men do."

Henry couldn't help wondering how proud Jim would be when he was hauled away in handcuffs.

Just then, Billy came bounding into the room. "Dad! I thought I heard you. I've missed you so much!"

"I've missed you, too," he replied, grabbing the boy up in his arms.

"Guess what, Dad!"

"I have no idea."

"Our Junior High Band is having a concert Friday night and I have a saxophone solo. Will you be able to come?"

"I wouldn't miss it for the world."

"Whoopie!" Billy yelled, and trotted back to

his video game.

"Well, I'd better get back to the kitchen," Ellen announced. "Jim, come give me a hand so that these kids can have some time together."

When they were alone, Henry held Marsha close. "I took part of my bonus money and got our house out of hock. We're not going to lose it after all."

"Oh, Henry," she cried, tears running down her cheeks. "I love you so much!"

"So you and Billy can come home --- if you want to, that is."

"Don't be silly! Of course we want to come home and be together as a family --- just like we used to. We'll move back tomorrow."

It was a bittersweet moment. It would be like it used to be --- at least for a few days, and then nothing would ever be the same again.

"You're doing WHAT?" Maggie exclaimed.

"It's not as dangerous as it sounds," I replied, trying my best to convince myself as well as my wife.

"All Willie and I are going to do is sit in a corner and play checkers."

My poor wife had endured a plethora of undercover operations --- everything from being declared dead so that I could stand in for a presidential candidate, to dressing as a transvestite and a candy-striper. She had mostly been supportive, but as more and more of these adventures had resulted in near-death experiences, I could see that her patience and tolerance were wearing thin.

"Oh, right! Just playing checkers! Surrounded by Neanderthals with snakes carved in their skin that just shot up your hotel with automatic weapons! Doesn't sound dangerous at all!"

I had to admit that it sounded different when she said it.

A few years ago, Maggie had been abducted by the Niners and was well acquainted with the violence and twisted minds of a street gang.

"I hear what you're saying, but whether we like it or not, those guys are out there and they're just going to get bigger and stronger unless somebody does something."

"But why does that someone always have to be YOU!" she moaned.

"It's not like we're going to be storming the place with guns blazing. I'll gladly leave all that to the Gang Unit. It's just checkers."

"You're impossible!" she said, with resignation. "What do we need to do to get you ready?"

"Well, I guess you noticed that I haven't shaved or bathed for a couple of days."

"Yeah, I noticed right after you crawled in bed last night," she said, wrinkling her nose. "I was planning on mentioning it this morning."

"All part of the cover," I replied, defending my personal hygiene. "Willie and I want to look like a couple of old street derelicts. We'll just blend into the wood work."

"So what are you wearing?"

"I found some old ratty jeans with patches and an old flannel shirt, and this!" I said proudly, holding up an old fedora that I had once worn to a Halloween party."

Just then, there was a knock on the door.

"Could you get that while I get dressed? It's probably Willie."

Maggie left the room shaking her head.

I threw on my bag-man clothes and crumpled fedora and joined Maggie and Willie in the living room.

Willie hadn't shaved for a few days either. His snow-white whiskers against his black skin made him look like a frail and emaciated Uncle Remus.

I glanced in the mirror as I walked by and noticed that I bore a striking resemblance to Festus on the old *Gunsmoke* TV series.

Maggie nearly keeled over laughing when she saw us together. "Well, at least I won't have to worry about you two old horn dogs picking up any women today."

"That bad, huh?"

"Honestly, the two of you are a disgrace to the homeless population."

"Sounds about right, then. Are you ready to go, partner?"

"Let's do dis!" he said with a grin.

Bruno's Blue Moon Bar & Grill was one of those seedy joints that respectable folks wouldn't dream of setting a foot in.

Its regular patrons were the down-and-outers that had to leave the shelters after breakfast every morning, hookers, and in this case, members of the local street gang.

When we walked in, I got a glimpse of the kitchen and wondered how the place ever passed its health inspection. After I was there a few minutes, I realized that it was probably because the health inspectors were afraid to come near the place. They probably figured that if anyone died of salmonella, it would either be a bum, a hooker or a gang member, and either way, it wasn't worth the risk.

We found a corner and set up our checkerboard.

I had just made my first move when the bartender came over. "This ain't no country club. Either order somethin' or hit the street!"

I looked at Willie. I hadn't actually ever seen him drink before.

"Wine," he replied. "Bring us de bottle."

The guy nodded and walked away. Willie hadn't specified what kind of wine. I remembered the wine list at the Melting Pot. They had over fifty different vintages and the least expensive started at about thirty bucks a bottle.

The bartender returned a few minutes later and plopped a bottle on the table between us. I noticed that he didn't bother to bring glasses.

The label read, 'Thunderbird'.

"How did he know what to bring?" I asked.

"You nevva heared o' Thunderbird? Dat's de black wino's bes' frien'."

An old guy at the next table overheard our conversation. "Guess you've never heard the Thunderbird poem?"

I shook my head.

"What's the word? Thunderbird!
What's the price? Sixty twice!
What's the reason? Grapes in season!
Who drinks the most? Them colored folks!
What's the reaction? Satisfaction!"

See, you learn something new every day.

Our attention was diverted when a curvaceous black woman in high heels and a skintight skirt that barely covered her hooha walked through the door. She took a seat at the bar and casually looked around the room.

I saw her spot Willie. She started to get off her stool and come our way, but Willie gave her a slight head shake and she returned to her seat at the bar.

"You know that woman?" I whispered.

"Sho do. Dat's Ginger. She's a workin' girl."

I figured that out the minute she walked in the door.

Somehow, Willie seems to be on a first name basis with quite a few Ladies of the Night. In fact, one of them, Maxine, had shared Thanksgiving dinner with us a few years ago. I once thought about asking him how these gals got on his speed dial, but decided that I really didn't want to know.

We had just finished our second game, when a couple of street punks wandered into the bar. I noticed the snake tattooed on the arm of one of the guys. It only had one fang.

He noticed Ginger right away and sidled up beside her. "How's it goin', gorgeous?"

"Just keep movin', Leon. You know I don't do no gang members."

"Thought you might make an exception fo' me," he said, rubbing his hand along her thigh.

She grabbed his hand and tossed it aside. "Nope! Don't do punks neither."

It was quite obvious that Leon didn't appreciate the put-down. "You got a smart mouth on you, little lady," he said raising his hand.

I saw Willie start to get up out of his chair and I put my hand on his arm. I seriously doubt that he would have heeded my warning, but fortunately, I never had to find out.

Just when things were starting to get dicey, another figure walked in the door.

"Leon! You raisin' a hand to a woman?"

"Rashon! Uhhh, no! Hell, no! We was jus' havin' a conversation."

It was obvious that Leon was completely cowed by Rashon's presence.

Rashon turned his attention to Ginger. He jerked his head toward the door and she immediately slid off the stool and headed out. As she passed our table, her eyes met Willie's and she gave him an imperceptible head shake.

"Looks like I need to teach you some manners, Leon. Now get yo' ass back to the pool table so we can talk."

He started to follow Leon, and then he spotted us. He walked up to our table and gave us the once-over. "Never seen you boys in here befo'"

I noticed that Rashon had cobras tattooed on both arms and each one had two fangs.

"Nevva been here befo'," Willie replied, taking a big drag of the Thunderbird. "We came into town on the Kansas City Southern from Dallas yesterday. Spent the night in de shelter. Some boys said dis was a good place to spen' some time. Looks like dey was right," he said taking another drag.

Rashon looked at me and back to Willie. "How come you can't find a black man to play checkers wit?"

"De man saved my ass from gettin' rolled by some junkies. I owe 'em."

I saw a smile curl on Rashon's lips. "Black an' white. Salt an' pepper. Looks like dis is a game of condiment checkers!"

I was sure that the other two Vipers had no clue what a condiment was, but they laughed heartily at their leader's joke.

Apparently sensing that we weren't a threat, Rashon motioned his boys back to the pool tables.

As I watched him walk away, my ass slowly unpuckered.

"Whew! That was close," I whispered.

Willie just gave me a wink.

For a while there was nothing to be heard from the gang but good-natured banter. Finally, one of the guys asked, "You heard anything from Darius since we sent him a message?"

"Nothin' yet, but he'll come around. If he don't, we may have to wing 'em next time."

The third member busted out laughing, "Did you see de look on dat old guy's face when de bullets started flyin'? I bet he hadn't moved dat fast in years."

I almost wished that I could have been there. Seeing old man Feeney dive for cover would have been worth the price of admission.

Rashon got serious. "Are we all set up for the next meeting?"

"We been passin' the word," Leon replied. "Dat ole garage ova' on St. John should be bustin' at the seams. All de guys want a piece of the action."

That was what we had been looking for.

I motioned to Willie. He threw a couple of bills on the table and we headed for the door.

We got what we wanted. No reason to push

our luck.

After all, I had promised Maggie that I would be careful, and like Leon, I didn't want to get crossways with the boss.

CHAPTER 12

As Henry Martin sat in the coffee shop waiting for 'Max' to pick him up, he reflected on the past two days.

Marsha and Billy had moved back into their home and things almost seemed normal again. He had attended Billy's Junior High concert and Billy had been so proud when he finished his solo and saw his Dad stand up and applaud.

Last night he and Marsha had made love for the first time in many weeks. His dismal failure as a father, husband and provider had carried over into the bedroom. The anxiety and pressure of their financial woes had made performing an impossible task.

Marsha had been understanding and supportive, but last night, as they lay in bed, sweaty and exhausted, Marsha had sighed, "My Henry is back. Tell your boss 'thanks' for me. You new job has saved our home and our marriage."

"For a few days, anyway," he had thought. He wondered how she would feel about his new job after he had completed his assignment.

Henry had been told to look for a black Hummer --- not many of them on the street. When one pulled up to the curb outside the coffee shop and tooted, Henry knew that from the minute he sat foot in that vehicle, his life would be changed forever.

He climbed into the passenger seat and was surprised --- no, shocked --- to see a young man, maybe thirty, in a tight-fitting black shirt. His head was shaved to the scalp and a Nazi swastika was tattooed on his upper arm.

"Max?"

The young man smiled. "You probably figured from the first time we spoke that Max wasn't my real name. You've taken our money and committed to your assignment, so we don't have to play games anymore. My name is Brant Jaeger."

Jaeger pulled out into traffic. "I imagine you have some questions."

"Skinheads? Am I to understand that I have been hired by Neo-Nazis?"

"That's a name that was bestowed upon us by the press, but essentially, yes. My organization is actually the Aryan Brotherhood Confederation. There are various groups scattered throughout the United States, but we have put aside our petty differences and joined together to make this bold statement."

"The assassination of the president?" Henry asked. "That's your statement?"

"Hardly," Jaeger replied. "The task we have assigned to you is just a piece of a larger picture --- a means to an end. Our goal has always been the implementation of the fourteen words."

This was a new one for Henry. "Fourteen words? What's that?"

"It is our motto --- our creed, 'WE MUST SECURE THE EXISTANCE OF OUR PEOPLE AND A FUTURE FOR WHITE CHILDREN.' Our country is being overrun with blacks, Asians, Muslims, Jews and Mexicans. Did you know that only 23% of the American population under eighteen is white? Did you know that four states in this country are already a majority of non-whites and 10% of all counties in the country are non-white? Did you know that only 3% of the world's population are white women of child-bearing age?"

Henry couldn't believe what he was hearing. "So your master plan is the extermination of everyone that's not lily white?"

"Extermination is a strong word, Henry. These people have a place in this world --- just not here in my country."

"Sounds like a losing battle to me."

"Indeed it is a battle, and we have just begun to fight. We will not rest until we have taken back our birthright."

Henry was beginning to have second thoughts. "If you're expecting me to embrace your cause, we may have a problem."

"We expect no such thing. Either you believe or you don't. It is not a prerequisite for your work. As far as we're concerned, you are a hired gun --- nothing more."

"Why me?"

"Because you are invisible. Mr. Nice Guy. Mr. Average American. No police record --- not even a parking ticket. Even with your recent financial problems, your taxes are paid. The most controversial organization you have ever belonged to is the Boy Scouts. The government doesn't care about you. My organization, on the other hand, is being constantly monitored by Big Brother. We couldn't get anywhere close to the president, but you can because you're Mr. Nice Guy."

The irony of the situation was not lost on Henry. He had been given the most despicable of acts because he was the least likely person to actually do it.

Henry noted that they were headed in a southerly direction.

"Where are we going and what happens when we get there?"

"You'll see soon enough," Jaeger replied. "We have an encampment about two hours south of Kansas City in St. Clair County, a few miles from a little burg called Roscoe. It won't do us any good to get you close to the president if you can't hit the broad side of a barn. We have some friends there that will give you instructions in the proper handling of firearms and you'll have plenty of time to practice. You may only have time for one shot. You'll have to make it count."

An hour and a half later, they passed Lowry City. The sign along the highway stated, 'Where the Ozarks meet the plains'. Sure enough, the fields of corn, soybeans and hay turned into forested hills.

They turned off of the highway onto County Road 'B' and headed west to County Road 'E'.

A few miles south on 'E', Jaeger pointed to a monument. "That's the spot where the Younger Brothers had a shootout with some Pinkerton agents. We're almost there."

A few miles further, Jaeger turned off on a gravel road.

"So do you guys own some land back in here?" Henry asked.

"Oh, heavens no. The Osage River is just through those trees. All this land is subject to flooding by the river. The land belongs to the Army Corps of Engineers. It's government land. We're citizens, so we figured we might as well use it."

After going another mile or so, Henry could see some smoke rising through the tall oak trees. As they got closer, he saw two-man lean-to's, just like in the old photos he had seen of the very early days at the Boy Scout Reservation.

When Jaeger pulled up to the edge of the camp, a dozen men materialized from behind tall oaks. Each of them was carrying some type of automatic rifle. Henry noticed right away that these men were not part of the Aryan Brotherhood. In fact, most of them had shoulder-length hair and scruffy beards.

"I'm guessing these guys are not Neo-Nazis."

"You're quite observant," Jaeger replied. "No, these gentlemen are members of the Ozark Militia. It just so happens that their agenda and ours coincide --- at least the part that involves the removal of the president."

"That's Terrance Cobb," Jaeger said, pointing to a tall rustic guy striding toward them. "He'll be taking care of you for the next week."

Cobb was the embodiment of Henry's mental picture of Daniel Boone or Davy Crockett.

Cobb extended a calloused hand as Henry stepped out of the Hummer.

"Welcome to the Roscoe Encampment. I hope you're up to roughing it for a few days."

"I'll manage," Henry said, taking his hand.

"He's all yours, Cobb," Jaeger said. "I have to get back to the city. I'll be back to pick him up one week from today. Think you can make a sharpshooter out of him in seven days?"

Cobb looked at Henry, "You'll think he's the second coming of Annie Oakley!"

"I hope so," Jaeger said, climbing into the big SUV. "We're counting on you."

"Hungry?" Cobb asked, as they watched Jaeger's dust rise from the gravel road. "We were about to have a bite of lunch. Hope you like fish. We've got a trot line out there in the Osage. We hunt or catch everything we eat. It's a survival skill that just might come in handy one of these days."

"Sure," Henry replied. "Fish is great. Do you serve fries with that?"

Cobb roared with laughter. "A sense of humor! Good! Just what this camp needs."

Henry and the twelve militiamen gathered around the smoldering coals of the campfire.

"Men, this is Henry Martin. We're gonna

make a hunter out of him."

After a lunch of seared catfish, Cobb took Henry to one of the lean-to's.

"This'll be your home for the next week. You'll want to gather some leaves for padding. Whatever makes you comfortable. The latrine is behind that big sycamore over there. There's a shovel leaning against the tree. Be sure to cover your business when you're through. Anybody forgets, we give 'em a special assignment."

Henry assured him that he wouldn't forget.

"Just make yourself comfortable, get your bed ready and meet the other guys for the rest of the day. We'll get started on your training right after breakfast."

That evening, as they sat around the campfire, Henry asked Cobb the question that had been haunting him all day. "You and your men seem so different from the Aryans. What brought your two groups together?"

"The Skinheads have their agenda. They hate everyone but themselves. We take more of a 'live and let live' point of view. Our problem is that this administration is going to do everything in its power to emasculate the Second Amendment. They want the guy out of the White House because they think he's gonna flood the country with immigrants. We want him out because he's trying to take our guns away. Either way, he's gotta go."

"I've noticed that most of your guys are carrying automatic rifles. Is that really necessary to pop a few squirrels or bring down a deer?"

"That's the argument that the gun control people are trying to make, but that's not what it's all about."

"Then what's it about?"

"It's about the right to protect ourselves from a tyrannical government."

"Surely you don't think ---?"

Before Henry could get the sentence out, Cobb was off and running.

"In 1935, Adolph Hitler wrote, '*For the first time in history does a nation have complete gun registration. Our streets will be safer, our police more efficient. The world will follow our lead in the future.*' Seven years later, after slaughtering and enslaving millions, he wrote, '*The most foolish mistake we could possibly make would be to permit the conquered Eastern peoples to have arms. History teaches us that all conquerors who have allowed their subject races to carry arms have prepared their own downfall by doing so*'. Did you know that our government is stockpiling hundreds of thousands of rounds of ammunition? Did you know that they have built hundreds of armored vehicles --- not for use overseas? Did you know that the president has said that he would not hesitate to use drones against American Citizens on American soil?"

"But this is the United States!" Henry protested.

"Exactly!" Cobb replied. "Thomas Jefferson and the founders of our country did not craft the

Second Amendment just to protect the rights of hunters and target shooters. It was included – right after the First Amendment guaranteeing free speech – to ensure the right of citizens to violently oppose a tyrannical federal government if need be. In fact, Jefferson wrote, *'The strongest reason for the people to retain the right to keep and bear arms is, as a last resort, to protect themselves against tyranny in government'*. We have every right to protect ourselves from those that would take away our freedoms. That's why we have made this unholy alliance with the Aryan Brotherhood, and that's why we are giving you a very large sum of money."

As Henry lay in his lean-to, listening to the tree frogs and locusts, he reflected on what he had heard from Jaeger and Cobb.

He certainly didn't buy into the hate-mongering of the Skinheads. In fact, some of his closest and dearest friends were black, Jewish and Latino.

He was more disturbed by what he had heard from Cobb. While he couldn't really get his head around the possibility that the government's agenda was to subjugate its citizens, he also remembered seeing newsreel footage of Adolph Hitler addressing huge crowds and being cheered on by German citizens not realizing that they were part of one of the most ghastly chapters in world history.

He also remembered seeing the movie, *Red Dawn*, where armed citizens fought valiantly against communist invaders. It didn't turn out well for the armed Americans.

If indeed the president were to send a drone in search of the Ozark militia, these hardy woodsmen, even with their automatic rifles, wouldn't stand a chance against the drone's missiles. There would be nothing left of Cobb's encampment but smoldering ash.

He realized that in any event, it wouldn't matter to him one way or the other. If he succeeded, he would soon be a prisoner of the state for the rest of his life.

The first rays of the morning sun were just penetrating the woodland glade when Henry heard men stirring around the camp and smelled the irresistible fragrance of sizzling bacon.

He groaned as he stumbled out of his thatched lean-to. It had been many years since he had slept on the hard ground.

"Mornin' bright eyes," Cobb said, as he watched Henry walk gingerly to the campfire. "Let's get you fed so that we can get started on your training."

"Somebody make a trip to the supermarket?" Henry said, looking at the pan of bacon."

Cobb roared again. "Supermarket? Another joke! I like this guy. No, Henry, a couple of the boys spotted a feral hog the other day. This is the last of the old boar. He's been mighty good eatin'!"

Henry wondered what other woodland delicacies might be waiting for him from Cobb's kitchen.

After breakfast, which Henry found surprisingly tasty, Cobb directed him to a path through the woods that opened into a grassy area next to a dry creek bed. Targets had been set up at various distances.

"You ever handle firearms before?" Cobb asked.

"I hunted with a .22 and a twelve gauge when I was a kid. Nothing recently, and I've never even held a pistol."

"Well, that's better than nothin'" Cobb replied. "Might as well get you started."

He handed Henry an automatic pistol. "This is a Glock 17. As the name implies, it holds seventeen rounds. That really don't matter much. You'll be lucky to get off one, maybe two rounds before the Secret Service boys have you on the ground. We're using this because it's an easy weapon for a beginner, but the 9mm cartridge has enough umph to get the job done."

Henry took the gun and just stared at it for a moment. With this weapon, he would take a human life and change the course of history forever. Life as he had known it, would be over.

Cobb could sense his student's hesitation. "Hey, I know what you're feelin'. It's scary as hell, but just keep in mind the bigger picture. I know about your situation. You're not doin' this because you believe in either of our causes. You're doin' it because you believe in your family and you're doin' what you have to do to take care of them, and I respect that."

Cobb had pushed the right buttons. It was all about his family.

"Then let's get going," Henry said. "How far away am I going to be?"

"We're going to try to get you somewhere between fifty and a hundred feet from the president. That's not an easy shot with a pistol, but we're not going to rest until we know you can pull it off."

Cobb showed Henry the proper stance and the two-handed grip. "Go ahead," he said. "Fire a round at the closest target. Let's see what you got."

Henry stood and pointed the gun as Cobb had directed and pulled the trigger. A hole appeared in the target a few inches outside the rings of the bull's eye.

"Well, at least you hit the paper," Cobb said. "That's a start."

Over the next few hours, Cobb instructed Henry on the details of firing the Glock, controlled breathing, sighting, and squeezing rather than pulling the trigger.

By lunchtime, Henry was putting the rounds into the bull's eye of the closest target consistently.

They had just returned to the campsite when two of the militiamen entered the clearing carrying a young buck.

"I thought deer season was a few months away," Henry observed.

"That's the government's deer season, not ours," Cobb replied. "Think of us as Robin and his Merry Men in Sherwood Forest. Like them, we don't kill for sport, or so we can hang a head with a big rack on our wall. We kill to eat. There are thousands of deer in these woods and the Sheriff of Nottingham isn't gonna miss the few we take to fill our bellies."

Henry watched with interest as the men hung the buck from a tree branch and slit the animal's throat.

As the blood drained from the carcass and soaked into the ground, Henry marveled at the ease with which some men could take the life of a living creature and he wondered if he would become one of those men.

He would know soon enough.

CHAPTER 13

After Willie and I left Bruno's Blue Moon Bar & Grill, I called the Captain and asked him to have Franco Harriman from the Gang Unit meet us at his office.

They were both waiting when we walked in the door.

"Got something for us?" Harriman asked eagerly.

I shared our morning's adventure including the fact that the Vipers had a meeting scheduled at an old garage somewhere on St. John Avenue.

"Any idea which garage?" he asked hopefully.

I shook my head.

"No matter," he replied. "There can't be that many vacant garages on St. John. I'll have a man sitting on every one of them. We'll find the bastards."

I had noticed that as I told my story, Harriman had scooted his chair as far away from me as possible. He had tried to do it inconspicuously, but it was actually quite obvious.

I had also noticed the Captain wrinkling his nose.

"I really appreciate how you and Willie embraced your roles as homeless derelicts. You're both quite authentic --- right down to the B.O. Take the rest of the day off. Go home. Take a shower. Burn your clothes."

"That bad, huh?"

"You have no idea!"

As we walked out the door, I saw the Captain pull a can of Glade Air Freshener out of his desk and liberally spray his office.

I had hoped that Maggie would be at the real estate office and I would have time to clean up before she came home, but no such luck.

She had taken the day off and had been pacing the floor worrying about Willie and me in the Cobra's den.

Willie went straight to his studio in the basement.

When I opened our apartment door, Maggie rushed over to give me a big hug, but stopped abruptly.

"Whoa! Are you ever ripe! I'm so glad you're okay, but no hugs or kisses until you shower."

I was about to strip down when there was a knock on the door.

When Maggie opened the door, a UPS driver was standing there with a package.

"Is this the William's residence?"

Maggie nodded.

"Sign here, please," he said, handing her a clipboard.

Maggie signed and took the package.

"Are you expecting anything?" she asked.

"Nope. Who's it from?"

"Pricilla's. Ever heard of it?"

The only Pricilla's that I knew of was a lingerie and novelty shop on Main Street.

Maggie got the scissors and opened the box. I saw the look of surprise on her face.

"Walt! If you wanted to spice up our love life, why didn't you just say so?"

"I have no idea what you're talking about," I said, as I walked over to view the contents of the box. "Our love life is just fine."

I, too, was shocked when I saw the package of edible panties and strawberry shortcake motion lotion.

We were both trying to figure it out when there was another knock on the door. It was Dad, Bernice and Jerry.

"Hi Son. I've been expecting a package. I don't suppose ---. Ohhh, there it is!" he said, spying the cardboard box. "You've opened it!"

"Well, it was addressed to Mr. Williams," Maggie said. "We didn't know that they meant the kinky one!"

'Kinky' was probably a fairly accurate description of my horny old man. I hadn't seen him for years until I got a call from a senior center in Arizona. Dad was being 'asked to leave' because of his lascivious behavior.

Shortly after moving into my building, he latched onto Bernice, another octogenarian tenant, and they have been an item ever since.

Anyone claiming that old folks are devoid of passion hasn't seen Dad and Bernice in action. They even got arrested for doing the nasty at the top of the World War I Memorial. They claimed that it was on their bucket list.

While Dad's libido may be chemically enhanced, it certainly hasn't withered away.

Dad grabbed the box from Maggie and examined the contents with Bernice looking over his shoulder.

"Ohhh, strawberry shortcake!" she gushed. "It'll be just like licking a big old strawberry popscicle!"

That was waaaay more information than I wanted. I desperately fought to erase the image from my mind.

Jerry had been standing back, taking in the whole scene with a big grin on his face. Seeing an opening, he couldn't resist.

"Sending stuff like that in the mail can be very risky. I heard about a shipment of Viagra that got hijacked on the way to the warehouse. The cops warned the public to be on the lookout for a gang of hardened criminals!"

"Sure glad that didn't happen to our stuff," Bernice interjected. Then she wrinkled her nose. "John, what's that awful smell? I think something might have died. You should have Willie look around."

Maggie had seen and heard enough.

"Out! All of you," she said, shooing them out

the door. "And take your toys with you!"

Then she turned her attention to me. "Hit the shower, buster. I may not have any strawberry shortcake, but I've got some Hershey's syrup and I'm in the mood for a chocolate long john."

That was the image that I was looking for!

The next morning after squad meeting, the Captain asked Ox and me to come to his office.

Franco Harriman was already there.

"Much better!" he declared, sniffing the air.

"Did you find the garage?" I asked, ignoring the barb.

"Yeah, we found it, but it didn't really do us much good. Our guys watched twenty or so gang members go into the place. We really couldn't do anything but watch. They weren't breaking any laws and we didn't have enough to ask for a search warrant. They broke up about ten o'clock and scattered. An hour later, a liquor store over on Prospect was hit. It was a Viper, probably earning a fang."

"Too bad," I said. "How can we help?"

The Captain and Harriman exchanged glances. "We need a man on the inside," Harriman said.

That one took me by surprise. On at least a

dozen different occasions, when I had been sitting in that chair and hearing those words, I was about to be volunteered for an undercover assignment.

"Please! You can't be serious! Do you really think an old white man could blend in with a gang of young black men?"

The Captain and Harriman both laughed. "Heavens no!" the captain replied. "There's not enough spray tan to darken your lily white skin and even if there was, I don't think that the second coming of Al Jolson would go over very well. We have something else in mind."

I waited expectantly.

"This Darius kid," Harriman said. "Didn't you say that the Vipers were trying to recruit him?"

"Yes. They want him for his lock picking skills. Wait! Surely you're not thinking of putting him in that hornet's nest. He's just a kid!"

"Don't get your panties in a wad," Harriman replied. "Think about it. Didn't you say you overheard this Rashon character say that if Darius didn't come around they might have to wing him next time?"

I nodded.

"Realistically, the only way that boy is going to have any peace is to leave town or if the Vipers are out of the picture. Why don't you have a talk with the boy and see what he has to say?"

Unfortunately, Harriman was probably right. On his own, poor Darius was a sitting duck.

I knew that before I talked to Darius, I would

have to talk to Willie, and I wasn't looking forward
to that conversation.

"So dey want de kid to join up wit de
Vipers?" Willie asked. "Den what?"

"They'll put a wire on him so they can hear
what goes on in their meeting in that old garage on
St. John. If they hear a job being planned, they can
wait for the Viper to show up. They'll have him cold
and have evidence to connect him to the gang."

"You know what happens to Darius if'n dey
find dat wire? He won't come out o' dat garage in
one piece, dat's what."

"The Gang Unit will be just a block away,
listening. If anything starts to go south, they'll crash
the place in a matter of minutes."

"You been dere befo'. How'd dat work fo'
you?"

Willie had a point. On more than one
occasion when I was undercover, the back-up guys
were one step behind the bad guys.

"Looks to me like Darius is between a rock
and a hard place. He wants no part of the gang, but
you know they won't leave him alone. You heard
Rashon say they might have to get rough with him to
convince him. Do you have any better ideas?"

A long silence.

122

"Guess I don't. Les' go talk to Emma an' Darius. It's up to dem anyway."

Emma and Darius sat quietly while I told them about what we had heard at the Blue Moon Bar & Grill, and what Franco Harriman of the Gang Unit was proposing.

When I had finished, I saw the tears well up in Emma's eyes. She knew what was coming.

"I gotta do it, Grandma," Darius said with resolve. "They ain't ever gonna give me any piece. I either gotta do it, or quit school and leave you --- and I ain't no quitter!"

I worked out the arrangement for Darius to meet with Harriman at a remote location to be fitted for the wire. The last thing we needed was for a Viper to see Darius with a cop.

When we were ready to leave, Willie said, "I be along directly. I need a minute."

As I walked out the door, I saw Willie embrace Darius and then Emma. He whispered something in her ear. She nodded and held him close.

I would never tell the Captain or Franco Harriman, but I knew that wherever Darius was going, Willie wouldn't be too far away.

If it was me going into that lion's den, that's what I would want.

CHAPTER 14

Henry saw the cloud of dust and heard the crunch of the gravel as Brant Jaeger's Hummer pulled into the Roscoe Encampment.

He climbed out, stretched, and took Terrance Cobb's hand. "Well, do we have a marksman?"

"Damn straight!" Cobb replied. "Told you I'd make an Annie Oakley out of him. He can put the whole clip in the red at a hundred feet."

"I'm not concerned about round #17. Is he dead on with round #1?"

"Dead on! He's as ready as he's gonna get."

Jaeger turned to Henry. "Well done! Looks liked we picked the right man."

"So what now?" Henry asked.

"Now I'm going to take you back to civilization --- real food --- flush toilets --- a bed with a mattress. I'll bet you've had your fill of the wilderness."

"Actually, it's been very refreshing. I've been battling the banks, the credit card companies and the utilities for so long, it was good just to be out here where all I had to worry about was not wiping my butt with poison ivy."

Cobb roared. "This guy was a hoot! I'm gonna miss him!"

Henry grew solemn. "Seriously, how much time do I have?"

"A few days," Jaeger replied. "The president will be coming to Kansas City to dedicate a new preschool for inner city kids. As soon as we have his itinerary, we'll contact you. Once we pick the ideal location, you'll want to be there early to save your spot. There will be thousands lined up to see the guy and I'll never understand why. He's eroding the very foundation of our freedom. Until we call you, just enjoy your remaining time with your family."

"One more question," Henry said. "I'm no politician, but saying I'm successful, what have you gained. It seems to me that the next guy is just more of the same."

"Very astute," Jaeger replied. "This thing is way bigger than just us. You have a counterpart on the west coast that will be taking care of that situation at the same time. We have gone to great lengths to find the perfect moment when we can kill two birds with one stone, so to speak. I'm sure you've given thought as to how history will remember you. While other assassins have been labeled murderers, if we succeed in our mission, you may just be hailed by future generations as one of the men that liberated our country from tyranny."

As unlikely as that sounded to Henry, he had made his bed and now he had to lay in it.

At Emma's insistence, Darius had requested that Ox and I be part of the surveillance team. I suspected that Willie had put her up to it.

The Captain agreed and Harriman reluctantly granted us temporary admittance into the Gang Unit.

Darius had been wired, and six of us sat in the back of an old bread truck that had been converted to a command center, listening as he made his first contact.

"Well, well," Rashon said. "If it ain't my home boy, Darius. What can we do for you, school boy?"

"Well, for starters, you can quit shootin' up the hotel. Damn near got me killed an' old man Feeney shit his pants."

"I knew it!" Rashon said, slapping his knee. "So you got my message loud and clear?"

"That's why I'm here. I figured that if I wanted to see my next birthday, I'd better throw in with you guys."

"Ohhh, he's good!" Harriman said. "A natural!"

"Now you'se talkin' some sense," Rashon said. "You ready to get started?"

"What you want me to do?"

"We havin' a meetin' tonight at Smitty's old garage over on St. John. You know the place?"

"Yeah, I know it."

"Good. Be there at seven sharp. I'm gonna show you how we can make some real money. Before you know it, you'll have your first fang and a wad of cash in your pocket."

"Sounds good to me!"

At six-thirty, we were set up a block and a half east of the old garage.

Gang members, some with their pants barely clinging to their butt cheeks, came drifting in.

Darius arrived just before seven as he had been instructed.

The snippets of conversation we heard initially were what one might expect from a gathering of street punks; bragging about their latest sexual conquest or the bag of weed they had scored.

Finally, we heard the unmistakable voice of Rashon Rippe. "Yo! Brothers! It seems dat the invitation that we sent to the Three Trails Hotel the other day got someone's attention. I want you to meet Darius. De man's got some skills dat we'll soon be usin'. Tonight, I want him to see how we operate. Billy! Front and center!"

"I'se here, Rashon."

"Billy, take three of the brothers and hit dat electronics store over on Troost. Me an' Darius will be watchin'."

"You got it!"

"Let's roll!" Rashon shouted.

"Well, crap!" Harriman said. "We got what we wanted. We can be there waiting when they hit that store, but I wasn't counting on Rashon throwing Darius' fat in the fire right away."

"That could be a problem," Ox replied. "When your guys hit the store, Rashon's gonna know that somebody tipped us off and his first suspect will be Darius."

"But we know there's going to be a hit," Harriman said. "We can't ignore that. Let's just hope that Rashon isn't that sharp, or if he is, we can get to them before something happens to Darius."

I certainly understood Harriman's dilemma, but I didn't like the odds.

If everything didn't go exactly right, Darius would be in deep trouble.

Harriman dispatched the Gang Unit to the electronics store on Troost. They were to remain out of sight until Billy and his home boys entered the store, at which point they would sweep in and collar the four gang members.

We knew that Rashon and Darius would be sitting somewhere close by to watch the action. We were parked in the bread truck, out of sight, a few blocks away.

Once we were set up, the tech twisted a few dials and we heard Rashon's voice.

"Watch closely, Darius. Dis is what we call a 'smash and grab'. Billy can handle disarmin' alarm systems, but he ain't worth shit picking locks, so he has to bash in the glass to get in. Dat sets off the alarm and dey got just a few minutes to grab as much stuff as they can befo' the cops show up. Dat's where you come into de picture. With you poppin' de lock, Billy can slip in an' shut off the alarm and nobody knows we're there. We can take all the time we need and clean out the place. Get the idea?"

Darius must have nodded in acknowledgement.

"Good! Now watch. Here come our guys."

The next voice we heard was the squad leader of the gang unit. "Okay, boys! They're in! Let's do this!"

All hell broke loose as we heard commands being shouted and the panicked voices of the gang members.

When things quieted down, we heard Rashon's angry voice. "Dat just ain't possible! No way de cops coulda got here dat fast unless --- unless dey knew in advance dat we was comin'."

Silence.

"The only way they coulda known was if someone tipped them off, an' dat just wasn't possible because nobody knew about de hit before de meeting."

Silence.

"If dat's true, den the only way they coulda known was if somebody was wearin' a wire. Darius, are you wearin' a wire?"

"Oh shit," Harriman exclaimed. "He's made him! Let's go!"

You could hear the venom in Rashon's voice.

"Darius! You a dead man!"

"We're not going to make it!" I moaned. "He'll be dead before we get there!"

Then another voice came through the speaker. "I wouldn't do that Rashon. Put down the gun!"

"Louie! What are you doin' here? You puttin' dat big lip o' yours where it don't belong!"

"Jus' lookin' out for a friend. Now put that thing away before I have to do something we'll both regret."

Apparently Louie the Lip had convinced Rashon that it would be better to comply and live to fight another day.

"Darius," Louie commanded, "get out o' de car and head down de street. Somebody waitin' for you dere."

We heard the car door open and shut.

"You gonna pay fo' dis, Louie," Rashon muttered.

"We'll see about dat," Louie replied. "Jus' stay away from my friends."

Our connection faded. The last thing we heard was the roar of an engine coming to life and the squeal of peeling rubber.

By the time we arrived on the scene, there was no one in sight.

When I arrived at home that night, I went straight to Willie's studio.

"Evenin', Mr. Walt."

"Busy night, Willie?"

"No idea what you talkin' about. Been right here all night."

"Sure you have. Where's Darius?"

"You know dat I respect you, Mr. Walt, but it's better you don't know. If'n you don't know den you can't tell nobody."

"But Willie, you know Rashon's going to come after him. He's in danger and he needs police protection."

"Yeah, how did dat work out for Darius tonight?"

I could see his point.

"He's somewhere safe where Rashon ain't gonna find him. It's better dat way."

"What about Louie?"

"Louie can take care of hisself. Don't you worry about him. Louie's got more street smarts in his little finger den Rashon's got in his whole body."

"Okay, but if you hear anything, you'll let me know. Deal?"

"Deal!" he said

As I lay in bed, I couldn't help but marvel that a young man, trying to do what was right, was still breathing, not because of the Kansas City Police, but because of two old street-savvy con men.

The next morning after squad meeting, I cornered the Captain.

"Have you heard anything from Harriman after our bust last night?"

"Yes," the Captain replied, "and I'm afraid none of it is good. It seems that the four bangers they collared at the electronics store are a lot more afraid of Rashon than they are of us. They aren't talking. After they got the four of them booked, Harriman hit Smitty's garage, but it looked like the Vipers had pulled up stakes and moved on. The place was cleaned out."

"So we're back to square one?"

"Looks like it. I don't suppose you have any idea where Darius is hiding?"

"Not a clue!" I replied truthfully. "You'll let me know if you hear anything?"

"Absolutely!"

Ox and I had just pulled out of the garage when my cell phone rang.

It was Willie. "Mr. Walt. It's Emma! Rashon's done took Emma!"

CHAPTER 15

"Easy, Willie! Just tell me what happened."

"I got a call from Mary over at de hotel. When she came out to get her paper dis mornin', dere was a note stuck to her door wif a big ole knife. De note said, 'Darius, I got your granny. Will trade even up --- you for her. I'll be in touch. If you want to see de ole lady again, you'll do as I say.' It was signed 'Rashon'."

"Pretty smart," I said. "He knew one of us would get the message to Darius. So what do you think?"

"I talked to Louie and we bof agree. Even if Darius was willin' to make de trade, Rashon ain't gonna let either one of 'em live."

"Any ideas?"

"Nope! Louie is doin' some checkin' around, but I doubt he'll find where Rashon's keepin' Emma. I'se real worried, Mr. Walt. You know dat Emma's mighty special to me."

"Yes, Willie. I know how important she is to you. Let me talk to the Captain and Franco Harriman. Maybe they can come up with something. You call me the minute you hear anything from Rashon. Okay?"

"Sho will. Rashon betta hope dat you guys find him befo' Louie and I do. He done gone too far dis time!"

Ox had overheard the conversation. "Back to the precinct?"

"Yes. We need to let the Captain know about this."

"What do you think Willie and Louie would do if they find Rashon first?"

"Whatever they have to. You know how protective that Willie has been with Maggie and me. Well now he's messing with the lady Willie's sleeping with. I wouldn't want to be in Rashon's shoes."

"Walt, Ox," the Captain said. "I didn't expect to see you back so soon. What's up?"

I told him about my conversation with Willie.

"Oh boy! This couldn't have come at a worse time!"

"What do you mean?" I asked. "There's no such thing as a 'good time' for something like this."

"That's true, but now is especially bad. I'm about to have a visitor. You might as well stick around for a family reunion."

"A what?"

Just then, there was a knock on the door.

"Come!" the Captain said, and in walked Mark Davenport, my half brother.

Until a year or so ago, I didn't even know that I had a half brother and neither did my father. Dad was an over-the-road trucker, and given his overactive libido, he had been keeping a girlfriend way out on the west side of Kansas. The woman got pregnant about the same time that Dad's route was changed. She raised the boy by herself and never told my father.

We may never have known if I hadn't been working a case involving a new Dr. Death practicing euthanasia in Kansas City. Mark was an F.B.I. agent at the time, and had come seeking a contact with Dr. Death for his ailing mother.

Since that initial contact, I had worked two different cases with Mark, who had transferred to Homeland Security. I couldn't imagine what had brought him to Kansas City again.

"Hi Walt, Ox," he said, taking my hand. "Good to see you both again."

"You too, Mark. I hope you're not back because we have more terrorists lurking around our fair city."

"I hope not, too," he said with a smile. "At least not for the next week. The president is coming to town. As you now well know, the Secret Service is part of Homeland Security. I'm here with the advance team to get everything ready for his arrival."

In one of my previous assignments, I learned what an organizational nightmare it was to prepare a city for a presidential visit. The route from the airport had to be mapped, all cross streets had to be blocked, man hole covers had to be welded shut and all standing mail boxes had to be removed. If it was to be an outside event, every building in the area had to be checked thoroughly.

"Wow! Where have I been? I didn't even know he was coming."

"Supposed to be a really big deal. Part of the president's plan is to make preschool available to every kid in the country. He's coming to cut the ribbon on one of the first new facilities. Our problem is that the school is in the inner city. Security is going to be a nightmare. We're going to need every man your chief can spare to cover the area."

So that's what the Captain meant when he said that Emma's abduction couldn't have come at a worse time. In terms of allocating manpower, the president would definitely trump the needs of an old woman.

"I'm sorry, Walt. I'll talk to Franco Harriman and we'll do everything possible to find Emma, but, as you can see, we're in kind of a bind here. In fact, since you've had experience working with Homeland Security, I will want you and Ox to help co-ordinate with Mark and his team."

Wonderful! At just the moment when my friend needed me the most, I was being dragged away to help protect a president that I didn't even vote for.

That evening, I met with Willie to let him know what had developed.

"Have you heard anything from Rashon?" I asked.

"Louie did. Got a call on his cell from de creep. He tole Louie dat if Darius didn' man up, he'd be finding' his granny in pieces."

"We have to try to stall him until we get this president thing out of the way. Have Louie give him a call. Have him tell Rashon that it would be wise to lay low. The place is going to be crawling with the Secret Service, Homeland Security and every cop in the city. Tell him that Darius will cooperate, but not until the heat is off."

"Might work," he replied. "But another part o' that message is dat he better not hurt a hair on my lady's head. Not if he wants to live."

I hoped that Rashon would co-operate, because I knew that Willie meant every word.

After he returned from the Roscoe Encampment, Henry Martin had told Marsha that his company was giving him a few days off after his grueling week of corporate training.

Each day, he spent every waking moment with his wife and son. It was a bittersweet time. Each time they did something, his first thought was that this would be the last time they would be together in this special way.

Marsha and Billy were thrilled that they had him all to themselves without the constant financial worries that had plagued him for the past months.

On more than one occasion, he considered the possibility of trying to extricate himself from his obligation so that he could stay with his family, but each time he remembered two things.

The first thing was that lonely night when he sat alone in the dark house after the lights had been shut off. His family was gone and what was left of his home was crumbling around him. That was his darkest moment and he never wanted to experience it again. One way or the other, he would lose his family. Better to lose them, leaving them financially secure, rather than leaving them destitute.

His second thought was always Jaeger's not-so-veiled threat that if Henry crossed them in any way, not only Billy and Marsha, but her parents too, would be in danger. After seeing the Skinheads and the militia first hand, he had no doubts that they would make good on their threats.

As his last hours of freedom ticked away, he thought that this must be what it was like for a man on death row, knowing the day and hour of his execution. At least the convict had the hope of a last minute reprieve right up to the minute that the chemicals coursed through his veins.

He knew that no such reprieve was possible for him.

Finally the call came that he had been dreading.

"Henry this is Jaeger. We have the president's itinerary. Are you ready to proceed?"

Henry heaved a big sigh. "Ready as I'll ever be. What do you want me to do?"

"Air Force One will be landing at KCI at noon the day after tomorrow. They will take I-29 into downtown Kansas City, get off on Independence Avenue, head east to Benton Boulevard and south two blocks to the new preschool. You'll want to get there plenty early. The streets all along the route will be packed. They have set up a stage in front of the new school. That's where the president will cut the ribbon and make a short speech. If you get there early enough, you should be able to get about seventy-five feet from the stage. The shot should be well within your range. Any questions?"

"No."

"One more thing," Jaeger said. "We haven't really talked about this before, but now is a good time. After the shot, when they take you, they'll want to know who you are working for. Tell them you were hired by the Freedom Fighters and that's all you know."

"Who are the Freedom Fighters? Is that what your coalition of groups is called?"

Jaeger laughed. "No, there is no such group. Our Brotherhood and the Militia are already under the microscope. The last thing we need is for the Feds to come storming after us. Freedom Fighters! Do you understand?"

"Yes, I understand."

"Good, because if we discover that you've ratted us out --- well, just remember Marsha, Billy, Jim and Ellen. We wouldn't want anything to happen to them, now would we? So are we good to go?"

"One last thing," Henry said. "Before I fire that shot, I have to know that the additional two hundred thousand has been deposited in my account. I'll be checking throughout the morning. When I see the money in the bank, then I'll be good to go."

"All business! That's what I like to hear. A deal's a deal. The money will be there."

After Jaeger hung up, Henry began the difficult task of writing the letter that he would leave for Marsha, giving her the information on the offshore account and the reasons behind his life-changing decision.

His final words were, "Please try not to hate me for what I've done. I love you both so much and I always will."

Fortunately, due to the fact that the president's ribbon-cutting was to take place right in the heart of Viper territory, Rashon saw the wisdom in laying low until all of the Secret Service and Homeland Security guys were off to another city and the K.C. cops were back to their regular beats.

As promised, Ox and I were assigned to work with Mark and his men, setting up the area surrounding the ribbon-cutting site.

City maintenance workers had erected barriers along the edge of the street from where the president's motorcade would leave the freeway, all the way to the new school.

The president wasn't due to arrive at the site until just before two in the afternoon, but all of us involved with security were on the job at daybreak. Even at that early hour, people were lining up behind the barrier to get a close look at the Commander-in-Chief.

I didn't envy Mark and his men. The neighborhood was indeed a security nightmare.

Older two-story buildings surrounded the new school. Each one had to be thoroughly checked out. As the morning progressed, I saw Secret Service snipers taking their places on the rooftops of the old buildings.

As before, when we worked with Homeland Security at the All Star Game, we were each fitted with microphones and ear buds so that we could communicate with Mark and his team in the command center.

By noon, every inch of space behind the barriers was taken. Most of the on-lookers were supporters of the president, but there were detractors as well.

Signs sprouted up with slogans like, 'Send the illegals back to their own country!' and 'Don't you dare touch my guns! I support the Second Amendment'.

Naturally, with time to kill before the arrival of the president, there were clashes between these two groups. Each time that the verbal jousting led to fists being thrown, cops in riot gear were johnny-on-the-spot to haul the combatants away in paddy wagons.

Mark was determined that nothing was going to mar the president's historic visit to Kansas City.

At one thirty, my ear bud crackled, "The president's motorcade has just turned off of I-29 onto Independence Avenue. They will be at the site in fifteen minutes."

The motorcade consisted of two SUV's leading the president's limo followed by two more SUV's. The five vehicles were surrounded by eight motorcycle cops.

The procession advanced along the route at a snail's pace, giving the president ample time to wave congenially to his constituents lining the street.

When the motorcade came to a stop, Secret Service agents poured out of the four SUV's, dressed in their black suits and dark glasses.

They surveyed the crowd for a full five minutes before the door was opened and the president stepped into the street.

He waved enthusiastically and raised his arms in victory as the crowd cheered.

He climbed onto the stage and took his place behind the podium. A contingent of U.S. Marines, followed by a school band, presented the colors and the Mayor led the crowd in the Pledge of Allegiance.

The band played the *Star Spangled Banner* followed by *Hail To The Chief*.

After their performance, members of the band dispersed, some of them racing to the concrete barriers where they met proud parents that had come to cheer them on.

The Mayor took the podium and talked for a good five minutes about how proud the city was to be honored with the president's visit.

Finally, the big moment came. The Mayor introduced the president and the crowd erupted in cheers once again.

When order had been restored, he spoke at length about his program to provide preschool to every child in America and how proud he was to be able to cut the ribbon for one of the first schools in his new program.

So far, the event had proceeded without a hitch. In just a few more minutes, the big guy would cut the ribbon, climb in the limo and be off to his next gig.

I was anxious for it to all be over so that we could get back to our normal routine. I had to figure a way to help Willie save his sweetie without any of us getting shot.

As Jaeger had suggested, Henry had arrived at the school early. It was a good thing, because he squeezed his way into the last opening at the edge of the barrier.

As he suspected, cops and Secret Service agents were everywhere, methodically surveying the crowd, looking for anything or anyone that might pose a threat to the president.

The cold steel of the Glock 17, pressed against his back and hidden under his light jacket, served as a constant reminder of the terrible act he was about to commit.

After what seemed an eternity, he saw the motorcade approaching. He pulled out his cell phone and accessed his offshore account. As promised, the money had been deposited. Jaeger had done his part and now it was his turn. It would all be over soon.

The president stepped out of the limo and after acknowledging the crowd's applause, climbed the stairs to the podium.

Henry hadn't really decided on the right time to fire the fatal shot. He figured that he would just play it by ear, depending on the circumstances.

Once the president took his place on the stage, he realized that he had made a tactical error. The president was seated directly behind the podium which blocked his view. When the president was to speak, only his head would be visible. Henry wasn't confident enough in his marksmanship to attempt a head shot. His best opportunity would be when the president stepped from behind the podium to cut the ribbon.

To his surprise, tears welled up in his eyes as

the Marines presented the Stars and Stripes and the band played the *Star Spangled Banner*. He had tried to convince himself that what he was about to do was for the good of the country. Jaeger and Cobb had certainly made convincing arguments to that effect. But as he watched the flag rippling in the breeze and heard the stirring words of the National Anthem, he knew without a doubt that what he was about to do was wrong.

Unfortunately, at that point there was no turning back. The money was in his account and if he didn't follow through, his family could well be dead before the day was over. He had made a pact with the devil and now it was time to give the devil his due.

After the last notes of *Hail To The Chief* had faded away, the band dispersed and kids were running in every direction.

His thoughts were focused on the president, when he heard, "Dad! Dad! Is that you?"

To his surprise, Billy came charging toward him.

"Billy! What are you doing here?"

"That was our band that was playing for the president."

"How could that be? You didn't tell me."

"We didn't know until early this morning. Another band was supposed to be here, but something happened and they couldn't make it. We played for the president, Dad! Isn't that cool?"

Henry could see the pride and enthusiasm in his son's eyes.

Now his son was going to have to witness his own father committing the most heinous of sins.

This was something he certainly hadn't counted on. It would have been one thing for his son to see the reports on the news as his father was being led away in handcuffs, but to actually see it in person, with the president bleeding and dying was unthinkable.

This development had changed everything.

"Billy, is your mother here?"

"Yes, she's back with the rest of the band."

"Then go to her right now. Do you understand?"

"But Dad, why can't I stay here with you?"

"Please, Billy. Just do as I say. I can't keep you here with me. Now go!"

"Ohhh, all right," Billy said, giving his Dad a hug.

After Billy had disappeared into the crowd, Henry looked around.

An older gray-haired cop was standing by a light pole on the other side of the barrier about ten feet away.

Henry muscled his way through the crowd and tapped the old cop on the shoulder.

"My name is Henry Martin. I have a Glock 17 in my pants and I was supposed to kill the president!"

CHAPTER 16

Just when I thought the ordeal was about to be over, I felt a tap on my shoulder.

A very common looking, thirty-something guy was standing behind me on the other side of the barrier.

I instantly saw the terror in his eyes, but it was his words that sent cold chills down my spine.

"My name is Henry Martin. I have a Glock 17 in my pants and I'm supposed to kill the president."

I didn't think, I just reacted. I pressed the button on my mike. "Mark, it's Walt. We've got a gun!"

I don't know what Mark said, but before the words were out of my mouth, the president was on the ground surrounded by the Secret Service.

A moment later, I heard the crack of a high-powered rifle and the slug hit the lamppost about a foot over my head.

At the sound of the shot, all hell broke loose. The crowd that had been pressed wall-to-wall against the barrier panicked. Screaming citizens scattered in every direction, some climbing over the barrier. There was no way that my fellow officers could contain the mad rush. The president's route that had been so carefully laid out was now filled with terror-stricken people running for their lives.

I heard a second shot and the slug slammed into the concrete barrier a few inches to the left of Henry Martin.

I grabbed Martin by the collar and drug him over and behind the barrier.

"Looks like someone out there isn't too happy with you."

"They said they'd kill me if I crossed them," he said, his face white as a ghost. "They must have planted a back-up in case I missed --- or for this."

"Let's take care of first things first," I said. "Why don't you give me the gun?"

"Sure," he said, pulling the Glock out of the back of his pants.

He had raised up just a bit to retrieve the gun and when he did another shot rang out, whizzing by his head.

I keyed my mike. "Mark! I thought you guys had the rooftops covered!"

"We did --- all around the perimeter. Those shots are coming from at least two hundred yards away. Must be some kind of sharpshooter. My guys are after him. Just keep your heads down. What's your situation?"

"No problems here. The guy has given me his gun."

"Copy that."

I turned to Henry Martin. "Who is behind all of this? Who is shooting at you?"

"Two groups that I know of, the Aryan Brotherhood and the Ozark Militia."

"Militia," I said. "That explains the sharpshooter."

"Look," Henry said, grabbing my sleeve. "I

don't care what happens to me at this point. They also said that if I screwed up they'd kill my family. My wife and son are here. They threatened my in-laws too. Is there anything you can do to protect them?"

"Of course we can," I replied, not actually knowing for sure. "You said Aryan Brotherhood. Are you talking Skinheads? Neo-Nazis?"

"Exactly! I've never seen so much hate bottled up inside someone."

An idea was beginning to form in my mind.

"Are these guys well financed? Do they have sophisticated equipment?"

"Well, they paid me two hundred and fifty grand to knock off the president and I've seen everything from automatic assault rifles to grenade launchers."

"And you're positive that they're going to come after you?"

"Absolutely!"

I pulled my cell phone out of my pocket and dialed Willie's number.

"Mr. Walt! You okay? We heared 'bout all the commotion on de TV."

"I'm fine. Listen, can you get a hold of Rashon?"

"Sho, but why?"

"How soon could you have Darius over to that old garage on St. John where the Vipers had their meeting?"

A pause.

"Louie says we could be dere in fifteen minutes. What you thinkin'?

"Call Rashon and tell him every cop in the city is busy protecting the president. This would be the perfect time for the exchange. Have him meet us there and make sure he brings Emma with him."

"Dat sounds kinda crazy to me!"

"It may be, Willie, but I think this is our best chance to get Emma and Darius out of this alive."

"You ain't been wrong befo'. We be dere."

At that moment, Mark came on the line. "Walt, my men have neutralized the sharpshooter. I think it's safe for you to come out now. I'll send somebody to pick up your guy."

"Mark, do you trust me?"

"What kind of question is that? Sure I trust you. Why do you ask?"

"Because there's a lot more of those guys out there that are involved in this assassination plot. I think I have a way to draw them out in the open. Also, they have threatened my guy's family. Can you spare a few men to watch out for them until we wrap this up?"

"Sure, that part's no problem," Mark replied. "What's the rest of your hair-brained scheme?"

"I need for you to have your guys stand down and let Henry and I leave the area."

"Walt! You've got to be kidding! That guy just came within a hair of shooting the president. We can't just let him waltz out of there!"

"You said that you trusted me and I'm saying

that Henry Martin is not a threat, but there are still very dangerous men out there that are. He can help us lure them out of the woodwork."

A long silence.

"I may get fired for this, but somehow your wacky ideas have worked out in the past. What do you want me to do?"

"First, I'm going to let Henry tell you about his family so that you can keep them safe. Then Henry and I will walk about six blocks north to St. John. There's an old abandoned garage there. Ask the Captain. He knows where it is. Give me a half hour and then hit the place with everything you've got. Just be careful. There will be several of us good guys in there."

"Heaven help us if you're wrong!" he replied.

I knew that what I had planned was a long shot.

If Lady Justice was to prevail, I wasn't opposed to a little help from heaven right about then.

Ox had been just a couple of hundred feet down the street when the first shot rang out.

I grabbed him and the three of us headed to Smitty's old garage.

On the way, I gave him the details of my plan.

"So any chance we have of coming out of this alive depends on these Skinhead guys coming after

Henry?"

"That's about it. He's got a quarter million dollars of their money and he's screwed them six ways from Sunday. They threatened to kill him if he crossed them in any way. I think the odds are in our favor."

"So how will these guys know where we are?"

"Come on, Ox. You're the guy that introduced me to all this fancy technology stuff when we were dealing with the Watchers. Henry has a cell phone and I'll bet dollars to donuts that they've been keeping an eye on him all day with a GPS tracker to make sure he was where he was supposed to be. Henry said these guys had sophisticated equipment."

"I certainly hope you're right!"

When we arrived at the garage, Willie, Louie and Darius were waiting outside.

"Any sign of the Vipers?" I asked.

"They already inside," Willie replied. "We saw 'em go in jus' befo' we pulled into de lot."

"So how we gonna play dis?" Louie asked. "And who is dis guy?"

"This is Henry. He's our ace in the hole. The five of us will go inside. Ox will stay out here out of sight just in case Rashon has some of his goons trying to circle in behind us."

"So we get inside?" Louie said. "What den?"

"Then we stall until our backup arrives."

"Dat's yo' plan! We all gonna get kilt!"

I could see the skeptical look on Willie's face,

but to his credit, he calmed his friend.

"Easy, Louie. I been knowing Mr. Walt a long time, an' if he says dis'll work, den it will work! I'se bettin' Emma's life on it."

I certainly hoped he was right.

Ox found a place out of sight and the five of us headed inside.

We paused for just a moment to let our eyes adjust to the dark interior. I spotted a stack of old tires along one wall.

"Over there," I whispered, motioning to the tires. "When the shooting starts, grab Emma and all of us will hunker down until it's over."

I saw Louie shake his head in dismay. I could certainly understand his skepticism.

We walked into the big room where the Vipers had held their meetings. Rashon was standing in the middle, surrounded by thugs holding automatic pistols and rifles. I counted at least a dozen men and those were just the ones that I could see. Emma was standing a few feet behind him.

"Well, well," Rashon said gleefully as he looked at our pitiful little contingent. "You all come here to make a deal?"

"That's why we're here," I replied.

Rashon took a closer look at Willie and me. "You those two old fools playin' checkers at de Blue Moon de other day!"

"Can't fool you," I said as sarcastically as I could muster, given the fact that I was about to wet my pants.

153

"An' you a cop on top o' that! Dis is betta dan I had hoped for. Which one of you guys is gonna get his fang for takin' out a cop?"

Naturally, every hand in the place shot up.

"We didn't come here to jawbone, Rashon. We came to deal. Darius for Emma. That's what you said you would do."

Rashon laughed so hard that he had to hold his sides. "Jus' what makes you think dat we gonna deal anything? I see an ole cop wit a .22 strapped to his side, his white-haired checker buddy, Fat-lipped Louie and the young punk dat ratted us out to de cops"

Then he spotted Henry. "Who is dat guy?"

"This is Henry. He is our ticket out of here."

Rashon took another look and laughed again. "If dis guy is your ticket, den you in big trouble. I'm thinkin' maybe it's time to just shoot ever last one o' you and I might as well start with your ticket there."

"I wouldn't do that!" came a voice from the back of the room. "That ticket is all mine!"

"Who is dat!" Rashon shouted. "Who you think you givin' orders to?"

A man with a clean-shaven head, wearing a black t-shirt and sporting a Nazi swastika on his arm stepped into the light where Rashon could see him. Behind him were a dozen more, all carrying automatic weapons.

"Holy shit!" Louie muttered and I saw Willie's eyes grow big as saucers.

No one said another word, but as the two

armed contingents stood staring at one another, you could see the hatred in their eyes.

It was the epic battle of the ages, the dog squaring off against the cat, the mongoose sparring with the cobra. No two groups on the face of the earth hated one another more. Black power versus white supremacy.

I could see that Rashon and the Skinhead were totally transfixed on one another.

I nodded to Willie and he nodded back. He broke away, grabbed Emma, and the six of us made a mad dash for the stack of old tires.

We had just made it to cover when the fireworks started. Automatic weapons erupted, bullets flew and the air was filled with the smell of gunpowder and the screams of dying men.

It probably only lasted a few minutes, but it seemed like an eternity before the echo of the last shot faded away.

I peeked around the stack of tires just in time to see Mark and his men sweep into the garage.

"Mark, over here." I said feebly. "It's us. Don't shoot!"

As Mark stood over our little group, he looked at the carnage strewn throughout the garage. "Walt, you're one crazy son-of-a-bitch!"

CHAPTER 17

As one might expect, the debriefing process involving a failed assassination attempt on the president dragged on until the wee hours of the morning.

Henry, of course, was taken into custody and the rest of us were transported downtown where we each had the opportunity to share our account of the events starting with Henry's tap on my shoulder and ending with the bloody shoot-out at Smitty's garage.

I learned from Mark that after the body count had been taken, Rashon Rippe and several of the Vipers were dead. Those that were still breathing would look forward to a very long stretch in the Leavenworth Federal Prison. For all intents and purposes, the Vipers, like the Niners before them, were a closed chapter in Kansas City's crime book. Emma, Darius, Louie and Willie were off the hook.

That was the good news.

The bad news was that Brant Jaeger's body was not among the fallen Neo-Nazis. Somehow he had escaped the hail of bullets from the Vipers. He was still at large somewhere in Kansas City and that meant that Henry Martin and his family were still at risk.

Given the fact that Henry had taken their money, failed to complete his assignment and was ultimately responsible for the death and incarceration of a dozen Skinheads, it was ludicrous to believe that Jaeger would not seek retribution.

My debriefing took the most time since I was involved from the very beginning to the bitter end, and since it was my 'hair-brained' idea to pit the Vipers against the Skinheads.

"What in the world made you think that you had any chance to pull this thing off?" Mark asked. "It was a long shot from the get-go."

I was almost embarrassed to share the thought process that set the whole thing in motion.

"Promise you won't laugh," I said.

Mark and the Captain nodded.

"Well, I remembered a sci-fi movie that I had seen --- I don't even remember the name. The hero was being chased by one of those velociraptors, you know, the little dinosaurs with a mouth full of teeth and long claws. Anyway, the hero tripped and fell. The raptor caught up with him and was just about to make a hero sandwich out of him when a tyrannosaurus rex appeared and snatched the raptor up in his huge jaws. That gave the hero just enough time to scramble to his feet and run into a cave."

I had expected some kind of response, but the two of them just sat there dumbfounded.

Finally Mark spoke. "So you're telling me that I put my career on the line because of an old movie you had seen?"

"Well, yeah. That plus the fact that I knew how much those two groups hated one another. I figured that if I could get them together, we had a pretty good chance. Rashon wanted Darius and Jaeger wanted Henry. They both wanted something so much, they were willing to throw caution to the wind. It worked, didn't it?"

"Holy crap!" Mark muttered. "I can't wait to write this up in my report to the president."

At two in the morning, I wearily climbed the steps to my apartment.

After the shootout, I had called Maggie to tell her I was okay and that I would probably be late due to the lengthy debriefing that I anticipated. I told her to go on to bed.

Naturally, when I opened the door I realized that she hadn't listened to a word I said. She had been waiting up for my return.

She rushed up and threw her arms around me. Then she backed away and punched me in the arm.

"Why?"

"Why what?" I asked bewildered.

"Why, out of hundreds of cops on that scene, did that lunatic choose YOU!"

"Well, first of all, he's not a lunatic ---."

"That's not my point! Why you? Why is it always you?"

"I wish I had an answer for you, Maggie," I said, pulling her back to me. "I don't go looking for these things. They just happen. Maybe we have to believe that something bigger than you and me is out there pulling some strings."

"I saw that horrible scene on TV," she said, sobbing, "and I knew that you were right in the middle of it. I was so scared."

"Yeah, me too," I said truthfully. "But here we are. I'm home and everybody that we care about is okay. That's what is important."

Later, as I lay in bed with Maggie curled up beside me, I replayed the day's events in my mind. I was home safe with the one I loved, Ox was at home with Judy and I was willing to bet that Willie was somewhere cuddling Emma. We had all made it through. It could have turned out a lot worse.

Then I thought about Henry Martin and his family. For them, the danger had just begun.

I slept until noon.

I had just finished my coffee and read about our ordeal in the paper when the phone rang. It was the Captain.

"Hi, Walt. I know you were supposed to have the day off, but I wonder if you could come down to the station. We've had some new developments and we'd like your input."

"Sure, I'll be there in an hour."

When I arrived, Mark, the Captain and another man I didn't recognize were waiting in the Captain's office.

"Walt, I'd like you to meet Dr. Wheeler. He's

a forensic psychologist and a profiler with the FBI."

After the introductions were over, the Captain got down to business.

"Brant Jaeger didn't waste any time coming after Henry Martin and his family. Both Henry's home and the home of Jim and Ellen Bennett, his in-laws, were torched last night. Fortunately, after hearing from you and Henry, Mark had taken Marsha, Billy and the Bennett's into protective custody and placed them in a safe house. Unfortunately, both homes were a total loss. Both families have lost everything."

"Holy crap!" I replied. "I figured this guy was dangerous. If he would go after a sitting president, I'm sure he would have no problem executing the guy that crossed him."

"Dr. Wheeler has been examining our case and has come up with a profile of the participants," the Captain said. "I'll let him explain and then we'd like your input."

"First," Dr. Wheeler began, "let me say that Brant Jaeger's concept was brilliant. He knew that his Aryan Brotherhood as well as the Ozark Militia, was being routinely scrutinized by Homeland Security."

Mark nodded in agreement.

"His plan was to choose a model citizen that would be far off of the government's watch list, but vulnerable. Henry Martin was the perfect choice.

"My department has looked into Martin's life and the man is squeaky clean --- not so much as a parking ticket. Unfortunately, Henry Martin and his family fell victim to the downturn in the economy and the outflow of American jobs to other countries. He was laid off when his firm relocated to Mexico and hasn't found work in over a year. He exhausted his savings, maxed out his credit cards and his home was going into foreclosure. His situation made him vulnerable. Jaeger's offer of two hundred and fifty thousand dollars was viewed as his families salvation."

"But still," Mark said, "what kind of man would agree to murder a president?"

"You are quite right, Mark, but you have just made the same mistake that Jaeger made. It is one thing to agree to such a horrific act and quite another to carry it out. One can only imagine the torment that Henry Martin must have felt as he saw his home and family crumbling around him. We, as arm chair quarterbacks, can sit back in judgment, but I'm reminded of the old Indian saying, 'Don't judge a man until you have walked a mile in his moccasins'. Any one of us in Henry Martin's situation may very well have done the same thing."

I found myself liking this FBI shrink. He was very down-to-earth.

"The thing that distinguishes men like Jaeger from men like Henry Martin is the sociopathic personality. The sociopath is characterized by a deep-seated rage, a lack of remorse, shame or guilt. They see others around them, not as people, but as targets and opportunities. They are manipulative and cunning and believe that only their way is the right way. They do not have the capacity to love and cannot empathize with the pain of their victims. Their brains are simply not wired to process such emotions. Jaeger is all of these things; Martin is none of them.

"Jaeger's plan did not take into account the one thing that would make it fail --- that Henry Martin possessed a conscience. In the final analysis, Henry simply couldn't pull that trigger."

"Now that you have heard Dr. Wheeler's analysis," the Captain said, "we'd like your input. You were with the man. How we proceed from here will be determined by whether we believe that Henry Martin can be trusted."

I had actually only been with the man for a few hours, but like soldiers in the trenches of war, you learn a lot about a man when lives are on the line.

I tried to choose my words carefully. "My association with Henry Martin was brief, but it was under extremely trying circumstances. My impression of the man coincides with Dr. Wheeler's analysis. I believe Henry loves his family and his country and I believe he can be trusted."

The three men looked at one another and nodded.

"That's our assessment, too, but we wanted your opinion. The success of our plan to bring Brant Jaeger to justice is predicated on trusting Henry Martin."

I just hoped that we had read the man correctly.

CHAPTER 18

After I left the Captain's office, I stopped by the break room for a cup of the sludge that passes for coffee in the squad room.

A few cops waiting to go on duty were there, and another man that I recognized as a crime beat reporter for the *Kansas City Star*. He was always hanging around, hoping for some tidbit of information that he could publish under his byline.

I had just poured my coffee when I heard the reporter exclaim, "Hey! Isn't that the old cop that saved the president?"

One of the officers nodded, and before I could escape, the reporter was on top of me with a recorder stuck in my face.

"Officer! What's it feel like to be a hero? Have you heard from the president since the incident? Were you ever in danger yourself?"

The last thing I wanted was publicity. The only reason that I was involved at all was because fate had me standing closer to Henry Martin than any other officer.

"I really don't care to comment," I said as graciously as possible.

The reporter, however, was one of those guys that couldn't take 'no' for an answer.

"But our readers want to know!" he protested.

I tried to move away but he stepped in front of me, bumping my arm, which sent half the contents of my cup streaming down the front of my shirt and pants.

"No comment!" I said more forcefully. "Now please move aside so that I can go to the restroom and clean up this mess."

"Sure! Sorry about that. I'll just wait here until you come back out. Maybe we can try this again."

"Not a chance," I muttered.

Unfortunately, when I entered the restroom, I came face-to-face with Officer Dooley. We're good friends, but Dooley never passes up an opportunity to put the screws to the old cop.

He took one look at the wet stain on the front of my pants. "Whoa! Did someone forget their Depends this morning?"

"Very funny! I have that creep reporter from the *Star* to thank for this."

"Yeah, he can be a real pain in the ass sometimes. Anything I can do to help?"

I looked around and spotted a window that opened onto a fire escape.

"Yeah, you can," I replied. "Help me get this window open. After I'm out of here, go out and tell the reporter that I've changed my mind and I'll give him the interview if he doesn't mind hanging around for a while."

"I like it!" Dooley said, grinning. "I'm betting he'll wait half a day if he thought he was going to get a story."

We pried the window open and I climbed out on the fire escape. The squad room was on the second floor on the backside of the building that faced an alley.

When my feet touched the ground, I was just a few feet from a homeless guy that was curled up against the wall with a paper bag clutched in his hand. An old backpack was lying beside him.

Naturally, the first thing he saw was my wet crotch. "Got me a package of Depends," he said, tapping his backpack. "Sell 'em to ya fer five bucks."

I tossed a five at the poor guy, knowing that it would probably buy him a couple of bottles of Thunderbird.

As I trudged down the alley to my car, it was comforting to know that if I ever became incontinent, I would have options.

Before I had left the apartment for my meeting with the Captain, Maggie and I had decided that we would go out for supper that evening.

I have found, during my three years on the force that when I have been subjected to a near-death experience, one of the things that helps me cope is comfort food. The ordeal with the Cobras and the Skinheads certainly qualified, and my favorite source of comfort food is Mel's Diner.

It's not Maggie's favorite place because nothing that Mel serves is healthy, but it tastes like a little bit of heaven. Nevertheless, Maggie agreed to go since, once again, I had nearly bought the farm, and because it was actually my turn to choose. She had chosen our last meal out, The Melting Pot.

She was dressed and ready to go when I walked in the door.

"Well, there's our local hero and TV star."

"Excuse me! What are you talking about?"

"I guess you haven't been watching the news," she replied. "You're on every station. Here let me show you."

She switched on the TV and even though the footage was jerky, I immediately recognized the scene of the president's attempted assassination.

"Here you come," she said.

After the first shot had been fired from the sniper, I had grabbed Henry and pulled him over the concrete barrier. Some enterprising citizen in the crowd had recorded everything from that moment forward on their cell phone.

The reporter said, "The police have not released the identity of the officer that saved the president, but reliable sources have told us that he is a three year veteran and the oldest officer on the force."

At that moment, I had just received the 'all clear' from Mark, and Henry and I stood up. The cell phone camera had captured a full frontal view of my face.

"Oh great!" I muttered. "That explains the reporter."

I told Maggie about the incident with the

obnoxious reporter.

"Are you sure you want to go out?" Maggie asked. "If someone recognizes you, we may not be able to eat in peace."

"But I'm starving," I moaned, "and I need comforting."

Then I had an idea.

I rummaged around in the closet and found a box of stuff that I had used on various undercover assignments.

At the very bottom, I found what I was looking for, a black handlebar moustache and a pair of bushy eyebrows to match.

The gooey stuff on the back seemed fresh enough, so I went into the bathroom mirror and stuck them on.

When I returned to the living room, Maggie giggled. "Well, you're not exactly Tom Selleck, but it might work."

Actually, I thought I looked more like Juan Valdez, the Columbian coffee guy, but they always picture him with a donkey so I figured I'd better not mention that to Maggie.

As we were walking out of the building, we met the Professor. "Well, well. If it isn't Juan Valdez."

I shook my head and put my finger to my lips.

"Juan who?" Maggie asked.

"Uhhh, never mind," the Professor stuttered. "Looks like the TV star is going incognito."

"I suppose you saw it too," I muttered.

"Seems like most everyone has seen it. Rejoice, Walt. This is your fifteen minutes of fame."

"That's about fifteen minutes too much," I replied.

"Ahhh, the irony," he said with a sigh. "Someone has said that a celebrity is someone who spends the first half of their life trying to become famous, and the second half wearing dark glasses so that no one will recognize them. I certainly hope your little charade works for you."

When we walked into the diner, Mel looked up from the counter. "Evenin', Maggie," he said with a wink. "Who's this handsome fella you're with tonight?"

"Juan somebody," she said shrugging her shoulders.

Mel laughed and handed Maggie a couple of menus. "Are you paying tonight or should I ask 'Juan for the money'?"

I never realized that Mel had a sense of humor.

I normally don't need the menu when I eat at Mel's. I have several favorites. I had already decided on a big chicken fried steak and mashed potatoes. Mel covers everything with the most scrumptious gravy I have ever tasted.

Nevertheless, I took a casual glance and noticed that there was a slip of paper clipped to the top. Mel does that when he has specials that are not on the regular menu.

The note said that Mel was serving his 'Smokin' Hot Pulled Pork Chili'. Now I had a real problem. My mind had been set on the gravy, but Mel's chili is a special treat. Instead of using ground beef, he smokes big pork butts and uses the hickory flavored pork. After a bitter struggle, I realized that I could get the gravy anytime, but the chili was a rare treat. The chili won. I would top it off with a big piece of lemon meringue pie.

Mel set the steaming bowl of chili in front of me and the aroma of smoked hickory made my mouth water.

It had been quite a while since I had this special dish and I had forgotten just how hot it actually was. I have to admit that I'm pretty much a light-weight when it comes to hot food. Tacos with mild sauce make me break out in a sweat.

I had consumed about half the bowl when the little trickles started running down the back of my neck. A few bites later, my forehead was wet.

I dipped in my spoon to take another bite and was shocked to see what looked like a caterpillar doing the backstroke in my bowl.

"Holy crap!" I exclaimed, showing the offensive creature to Maggie.

She looked in the bowl, and then she looked at me and laughed so hard that she snorted little pieces of her salad out her nose.

"What? What's so funny about that?" I said, indignantly.

She couldn't stop laughing. She just pointed at my head. "It's your eyebrow, goofy."

I felt, and sure enough, one of my bushy brows was gone. Then something else caught my eye. I felt my upper lip and discovered that my moustache was hanging half off.

It was pretty evident that my disguise was no match for the heat in Mel's chili.

"Take that stuff off," Maggie giggled. "You look absolutely silly."

I peeled off my half-moustache and remaining eyebrow and stuffed them in my pocket.

I had just fished the errant eyebrow out of the chili bowl and was wiping it with a napkin, when I heard, "Hey! Isn't that the old cop that saved the president?"

"Yeah, that's him!" somebody answered.

Before I could even stuff the eyebrow in my pocket, our booth was surrounded.

A guy thrust one of Mel's napkins in my face. "Hey, man. How about an autograph?"

Another woman plopped her baby in my lap and started snapping pictures with her cell phone.

Thankfully, Mel came to my rescue. "Hey, let's give the man a break. He's had a tough week."

Mel is a big guy and he didn't have to ask twice.

As the crowd dispersed, I handed him a

twenty. "Thanks for that. Keep the change."

He pushed the twenty back to me. "It's on the house tonight. You're my hero too."

As I walked back to the car, a thousand thoughts were running through my mind, but the thing that distressed me most was that I didn't get my lemon meringue pie.

The next morning, the Captain summoned me into his office.

I was surprised to see Mark Davenport back in town.

"Hi Walt. I thought we should get together so that I could catch you up on a few things."

I figured right away that Mark actually wanted something. Homeland Security didn't normally keep me in the loop.

"We've been working with Henry Martin trying to round up the remainder of the coalition that ordered the assassination attempt. He had told us about the Ozark Militia and how they trained him for a week at a camp near Roscoe about a two hour drive from here."

I knew Roscoe fairly well. Willie and I had spent some time there on another case.

"The militia was led by a fellow named Terrance Cobb," Mark continued. "Henry led us to the woods where they had their encampment, but they had pulled up stakes and moved on. The place looked like nobody had ever been there. They even spread dry leaves and branches over the spot where they had dug their latrine. We think they have probably moved farther south, maybe even into Arkansas. We've heard that there's another militia hiding in the Boston Mountains. They may have joined forces.

"Also, your timing was perfect. We were able to make contact with the agents that were protecting the vice president in California. They were able to get him away before any shots were fired. Unfortunately, we weren't able to locate Henry's counterpart out there."

This was all very interesting, but I didn't see what it had to do with me. I was waiting for the other shoe to drop. Finally, it did."

"I have some good news for you," Mark said. "I've been with the president and he was very impressed with your quick action the other day. He would like to fly you to Washington so that he can thank you personally."

I'm sure that he was hoping that I would be jumping up and down with glee, but my reaction was just the opposite.

"Look, I appreciate the gesture very much, but I'm just not into all of this publicity stuff. My mug was on TV yesterday and I haven't had a moment's peace. If you don't mind, just tell the president, 'thanks', but I'll pass."

Mark and the Captain couldn't believe what they were hearing.

"Walt!" Mark exclaimed. "You can't just blow off the President of the United States!"

What I wanted to say was that as far as I knew this was still a free country and that I could blow off anybody I chose, but I didn't.

"I'm not a hero. I was just the guy standing at the wrong place at the right time. It could have been any man on the force. Frankly, I'm not real excited about giving the guy another photo op for the press."

"Ahhh, so this is a political statement!" Mark said.

"Mark, let me remind you that you recruited me to work undercover with Ben Foster in the presidential campaign. I spent four months of my life campaigning with him against this guy and the other candidate. At first, I did it because it was my job, but the more time I spent with him, the more I came to believe in what Ben Foster stood for.

"Think about this. You recruited me because I was Ben Foster's double. That hasn't changed. If I'm in Washington, glad-handing the president, some reporter is going to remember, and the whole nasty business surrounding Ben's death will come up. I don't think the president would want that."

Mark thought for a moment. "We didn't think of that. You might be right. I'll take care of it. Jesus, Walt. There are people in this country that would give anything for an audience with the president."

"I'm sure you're right," I replied, "but there

173

are also people that feel exactly the opposite, people like Brant Jaeger and this Terrance Copper."

"That brings us to the other reason that we asked you to come in this morning. As long as Jaeger is out there, not only the president, but Henry and his family are in danger. We have to do something to lure him out into the open."

"I suppose you have an idea about that," I replied, suspecting that it involved me.

"We do," the Captain replied, "but after hearing how you feel about being in the limelight, you may not be interested."

"Let's hear it."

"At this point, Jaeger has no idea where Henry and his family are staying," the Captain said. "We want to give him the opportunity to find out. The press has been clamoring for us to make a statement about the assassination attempt and identify the shooter and the hero cop. We have held off, but now we see this as an opportunity to lure Jaeger into the open."

"Sounds like you're saying that Henry and I are going to be the bait."

"We've made arrangements for a press conference that will be attended by virtually every TV station in town. One of the news anchors will conduct an interview with you and Henry --- that is, if you're willing. There's no way that Jaeger could miss it. He'll know where you both are and if he does what we think he'll do, he'll follow you from the press conference to the safe house. When he tries to make a move, we'll be waiting for him. What do you think?"

"Like I said, I'm no hero and the last thing I want is media attention, but this is part of the job. I get it. I saw the hate in Jaeger's eyes and if this will get the guy off of the street, then I guess that I'm in."

"We were hoping you would say that. It's our best shot."

It was beginning to look like I was going to be a celebrity whether I wanted to or not.

CHAPTER 19

The plan was pretty straightforward.

An attempted assassination of the President of the United States was front-page news all over the country and people were eager to know everything about the man that was a trigger's pull away from changing the course of American history.

The Captain had said that a proposed news conference would be attended by every TV station in town, but once word got out, reporters from every major newspaper across the country flocked into the city, and all the major networks sent teams to relay the broadcast to their viewers.

There was no possible way that Brant Jaeger and the powerful interests that had bankrolled him could miss the event.

Henry Martin had agreed to bare his soul and tell his story from the day he lost his job which started the downward spiral of his family, until the very moment when he tapped me on the shoulder and surrendered his Glock. He had been instructed to share every minute detail, especially naming names and pinpointing locations. The whole production was orchestrated to infuriate the ego-driven Neo-Nazi and draw him out into the open.

Knowing the location of Henry's broadcast, it was hoped that Jaeger and his skinhead minions would follow Henry after the news conference in an attempt to discover the safe house where his family was being sequestered.

Even though I had tried to downplay my part in the whole affair, the public wanted to know more about the old cop that was standing under the light pole when history was being made. I would be at Henry's side during the interview to add my two cents worth to the proceedings.

After the interview, an armed escort would take Henry and me to a safe house where Marsha, Billie and the Bennett's were supposed to be staying, only they actually wouldn't be there. This safe house would be a decoy, right down to the department having a policewoman on site, pretending to be Marsha, to give Henry a hug when he walked in the door. If and when Jaeger attacked the house, Henry's family would be miles away.

Naturally, with any operation, there are a thousand things that could go wrong. We were counting on the fact that Jaeger would want to punish Henry by attacking his whole family. It was always a possibility that he could be laying in wait somewhere along our route with one of the grenade launchers that Henry had seen in Terrance Cobb's arsenal.

I had been on the receiving end of a grenade launcher twice in the past year and witnessed it's destructive power, so if that was, indeed, part of Jaeger's plan, we could kiss our tushies goodbye.

Everyone acknowledged that the plan was far from foolproof, but it was our best option.

As expected, Maggie was less than enthusiastic about Homeland Security dangling me as bait --- again.

"I'm beginning to think that your half-brother is trying to get rid of you!" she said with disgust. "You're like a little lamb being staked out for the wolves!"

"Well this wolf tried to kill the president. While I'm not his biggest fan, there's just some things we don't do in this country and if I can help put this hate-monger away, then it's the least that I can do."

"If you get shot --- or worse," she said, biting her lip to keep from crying, "I'll never forgive you or your stupid brother!"

Naturally, when everyone in my building heard that I was going to be on national TV, they were all a-twitter.

Rather than having to tell the story a half-dozen times, I gathered my little group of friends and family together to give them the details.

As far as they knew, the whole production was for publicity purposes. The last thing I wanted was for them to know that I was part of the bait that was to lure a homicidal lunatic out of hiding.

Dad, of course, was the proud father. "Who woulda ever figured that my son would save the president? I didn't vote for the guy, but it still wouldn't be right to see him shot."

"Dad," I protested, "I didn't save anybody. I was just the guy that he handed the gun to."

"Nonsense," he replied. "As far as I'm concerned, you saved the president."

"Oh my!" Bernice wailed. "Somebody tried to shoot the president? Is Mr. Kennedy okay?"

Apparently, as far as politics was concerned, poor Bernice was still somewhere in the sixties.

Mary reported that my newfound celebrity has caused some concern around the Three Trails. "Old man Feeney asked me if you was gonna raise the rent now that you was famous. I told him 'no', but then I pointed to those bullet holes in the front and told him if he didn't pay his forty bucks on time, you'd send the guy back over to remind him. You shoulda seen him skedaddle!"

After our little group disbanded, Willie pulled me aside.

"Didn' wanna say nothin' while everbody was aroun', but seems to me dat dere might be a bit mo' dan you was tellin' us."

It's hard to pull the wool over Willie's eyes.

I certainly didn't want to lie to my best friend.

"Actually, there is. We're hoping this broadcast will piss off this Jaeger guy and bring him out of the woodwork. Please keep it to yourself. No point in worrying anyone."

"I figured. I won't say nothin'. You jes be careful."

'Careful' was definitely part of my plan. I just hoped that it would turn out that way.

On the day of the big broadcast, Mark Davenport met with Henry's family and explained the plan.

"Until this is all over," he said, "it is of utmost importance that you stay hidden in the safe house. You must not go out for any reason. Do not contact anyone. We will be in touch with our agent here at all times. If you need to get a message to Henry or to me, just tell the agent."

Marsha saw the disappointment on Billy's face. "What's wrong, Billy? You look upset."

"Awww, nothing. Today is Jack's birthday and he had invited a bunch of us to a laser tag party. Guess I'll have to miss it."

"I'm so sorry, honey. As soon as this is all over, we'll have a laser tag party of our own just to celebrate."

That brought a smile to Billy's face.

Henry hugged his family and climbed into the SUV with Mark Davenport.

He hoped that the next time he saw them, the nightmare would be over.

Brant Jaeger listened intently to the voice in his cell phone.

"Yes, sir. I understand completely. Yes, sir, we have everything we need. We'll take care of it, I promise."

After hanging up, he turned to his five companions. "The fools think this little charade will lure us into their trap, but we'll have a surprise for them. Jocco, you keep your eyes on that screen. The minute you see something, let me know. Now we'll just turn on the TV and see what this coward has to say."

Willie and Louie the Lip were sitting in Louie's old Cadillac outside the Blue Bayou Bar & Grill.

"So if I'm hearin' you right," Louie said, "De Feds are hopin' dat dis Skinhead fellow will be so pissed dat he will follow 'em from de TV station to de safe house and they'll be waitin' for 'em when dey makes der move, only de family ain't der. Dey's moved 'em somewhere else."

"Das wot I'm figurin'. Sounds kinda lame to me. Whadda you think?"

"Well," Louie replied, "I'm thinkin' dat if dese Skinheads have any smarts at all, dey ain't gonna bite. You got any idea where de real safe house is?"

"Sho do. Mr. Walt tole me befo' he took off

to de TV station. He said if anything went wrong, at least de man's family would be safe."

"So how you feel 'bout dat?"

"I'd feel a whole lot betta if we had a back-up plan just in case."

"Got me an idea," Louie said, putting the old Caddy in gear, "but we gonna need some help."

I walked in the door to the TV station about forty-five minutes before we were to go on the air.

A bright-eyed little gal named Sherry met me.

"Mr. Williams, follow me. We need to get you into make-up right away."

"Make-up? What on earth for?"

"All those bright lights. We wouldn't want you to have a shiny nose, now would we?"

"Of course not."

Henry and the TV anchorman that would be conducting the interview were already in chairs draped in plastic gowns. A couple of gals that reminded me of Frenchy and Rizzo from the movie, *Grease,* were busy applying the various creams and powders.

A third gal with pink hair and a lip stud plopped me into a chair and covered me with plastic.

She opened a jar of goo and put a big glob on her fingers.

"What's that for?" I asked skeptically.

"This'll fill in all those pesky old wrinkles," she replied.

"Hold off on that," the anchor guy said. "Leave the wrinkles. Part of the charm of this story is that the cop that saved the president is the oldest guy on the force."

"I didn't save the president!" I protested for the umpteenth time.

"As far as the public is concerned," he replied, "yes you did. People love to love their heroes. Let's don't spoil it for them."

"Swell."

After I was powdered, the three of us were led to the studio. Sherry was right. The lights were definitely bright, and my nose, left unpowdered, would definitely have shined.

"Here's how it will go," the anchor said. "I'll introduce you both and then I'll ask Henry to tell his story. Take your time and don't leave anything out. The nation has been chomping at the bit to have a chance to hear directly from the man that agreed to assassinate the president. I may interrupt from time to time to ask one or both of you a question. After you finish, we'll open the phone lines very briefly to give the public the opportunity to ask you questions."

We both nodded.

A guy standing beside one of the cameras held up his hand and signaled, five, four, three, two one. We were on the air!

As promised, the anchor introduced us and

Henry launched into his remarkable story.

He recounted the trials and tribulations that his family had faced, and at the point where his family was gone and he was sitting alone in his darkened house, there wasn't a dry eye in the studio.

I'm sure that people all over America were wondering what they would have done if they had been in Henry's shoes when Jaeger called and offered a quarter of a million dollars.

After he had described how he had met both the Aryan Brotherhood and the Ozark Militia, the anchor asked him to characterize both groups.

"Actually, the militia guys were pretty nice. They appeared to be hard working country folk that had somehow lost faith that their government was acting in their best interests. Each one of them had grown up with guns and hunting. It was part of their culture. They feared that this administration was determined to take away their guns. We sometimes hear people jokingly say that you can take my gun when you pry it from my cold, dead hand. That was very real to them. I believe that they were acting out of fear --- fear that they were going to lose their Second Amendment rights."

"How does that compare to the Aryan Brotherhood?" the anchor asked.

"To me, it was the difference between fear and hate. They seemed to hate and distrust pretty much anyone that was not a white, Anglo-American Christian. Latino, black, Asian, Jew or Muslim, they were all the same."

"It was a very large sum of money that was offered to you," the anchor said. "Do you have any idea who was financing the operation?"

"Not a clue. They never mentioned anyone and I never asked."

"I have one last question, Henry. You stated that you were prepared to do what you had been paid to do right up to the moment when your son ran up to you. The question that everyone wants to know is if Billy hadn't come by at that exact moment, would you have pulled the trigger?"

Henry sat deep in thought. He finally looked directly into the camera. "I guess we'll never really know, will we?"

The anchor turned to me. "You've had quite an adventure, Mr. Williams. What can you tell us about your experience?"

"Not much, really," I replied. "I was just one of several hundred officers that were there for crowd control. I just happened to be the guy closest to Henry."

"Were you ever in fear for your life?"

"Certainly not from Henry," I replied. "He handed his gun to me right away and complied with every request. Things did get a little dicey when the sniper started firing at us."

"What can you tell us about the shootout that occurred a few blocks from the school?"

"It was just one of those circumstances where two cases seemed to intersect. I had white supremacists on one hand and black gangbangers on the other. It was kind of like mixing baking soda and vinegar. I figured that if I got them together, something would pop, and fortunately, it did."

"One last question for you. You're sixty-nine years old. Are you ready to hang up your badge and go out in a blaze of glory?"

"Heck no," I replied. "I'm just getting started!"

"Thank you both," the anchor said. "Let's open the phone lines and get some questions from our viewers."

As expected, most of the callers were idiots asking asinine questions. After a half-dozen or so, the anchor said, "Let's take one last call."

I saw the look of horror on Henry's face, when the electronically enhanced voice that he had described came on the line.

"Henry, you're a dead man and your family too. None of you will see another sunrise!"

The anchor made the 'cut' sign and the director went to commercial.

We had dangled the bait and the fish had bit. Now it was time to set the hook.

CHAPTER 20

In the real safe house on Anderson Street, the Bennett's, Marsha, Billy and the lone agent that had been left to guard them were huddled around the TV.

As Henry told his heart-wrenching story, tears streamed down Marsha's face. Her mother was beside her with a comforting arm around her shoulder.

"I might have done the same thing if I was in his shoes," Jim Bennett muttered. "A hard working, honest man just shouldn't be put in a position where he has to make such choices. Seems like the country's going to hell in a hand basket!"

Little Billy really didn't understand the ramifications of his father's actions and was totally unaware of the part he had played in the unfolding drama. All he knew was that he wanted his family back together and life to return to normal. He would have much rather been at Jack's party than holed up in a strange house watching a boring TV show.

Suddenly, he felt the urgent call of nature and slipped away from his mother's side.

"Where are you going, Billy?"

"I just need to go to the bathroom. I'll be right back."

After he had taken care of business, he spied his mother's purse on the dresser. He knew that her cell phone would be in the little pouch on the side.

The Homeland Security guy had told them not to call anyone, but he didn't say anything about texts.

A text wasn't really a call.

He found the phone and pushed the button to power it up. His text was short and sweet:

Jack, sorry I can't come to your laser tag party.
Have a happy birthday.
Billy

Without powering it off, he slipped it back into his mother's purse.

"Got it!" Jocco yelled.

Brant Jaeger rushed to his side and gazed at the glowing screen.

"Anderson Street! That's the break we've been waiting for. I'm surprised that Homeland didn't confiscate all their cell phones. Surely they know that we have GPS tracking."

"So what now?" Jocco asked.

"We'll all go to the Anderson house. After we take care of the guard, you and two of the boys will take the wife, the old couple and the kid over to our place on Troost. Me and the other two will wait at the Anderson place. When we don't show up at the fake safe house, they'll eventually give up and head back to where they know their family is tucked away safe and sound. We'll take them by surprise and bring them to Troost for a big family reunion --- their last!"

Willie, Louie the Lip and Darius were sitting in Louie's old Cadillac a block from the Anderson safe house when two SUV's rolled up.

Three men jumped out of each vehicle, half going to the front door and the other three circling around back.

Each group had one of the battering rams that the cops use to breech locked doors.

The intruders wasted no time smashing the door and a moment later, they heard a shot.

"Musta got the guard," Louie said.

A few moments later, they saw three of the men push Martha, Billy and the Bennets into one of the SUV's.

"Dis ain't goin' at all like Mr. Walt tole me," Willie muttered.

"Looks like half of 'em is takin' de family off somewhere else," Louie said, "an' de other three is gonna wait for the husband an' Walt to show up. You betta call Mr. Walt."

Willie dialed Walt's number on his cell. "No answer went straight to voice mail. If he's still doin' dat TV thing, he probably shut it off."

"You got de number fo' dat Homeland Security guy?" Louie asked.

"Nope, Mr. Walt never give me dat."

"You could call 911," Darius suggested.

"No 911 operator is gonna know nothin' 'bout a Homeland Security safe house," Louie replied. " By de time dey figure out what'd goin' on, ever thing is gonna be over and folks is gonna be dead. We better follow dat SUV. We can keep trying to call Mr. Walt."

Louie fired up the Caddy and made a u-turn. They stayed just close enough to keep the tail lights of the SUV in sight. Finally the SUV pulled up in front of a darkened building on Troost.

"I know dat place," Louie said. "Used to be one o' dem Payday Loan places. Rip-off joint fo' sure. Closed up a few months back."

They watched the three men shove their four prisoners through the front door.

"Try Mr. Walt again," Louie suggested.

Willie dialed, but no answer.

Louie sat deep in thought for a minute. "Got me an idea," he said.

He turned around and headed back to a Pizza Hut they had passed a few blocks back.

After the telecast, Mark met us in the lobby.

"From the sound of that last call, I'd say we got Mr. Jaeger's attention. Here's the plan. If Jaeger is watching, we want security to be just tight enough so that he won't suspect anything, but not enough to scare him off. Walt, you'll drive Henry in one car and I'll be right behind you in another vehicle. I'll have agents in several unmarked cars parked along the route to the safe house to see if we've picked up any tails. If they don't hit us by the time we get there, I'll drop you off and we'll just dig in and wait to see what happens. You could just hear the hate in his voice. I can't believe that he won't come after Henry."

As we drove through town, I expected at any moment to see a grenade whistling toward our car. Actually, I was hoping that I wouldn't see it coming. I figured that way it would all be over before we knew what hit us.

Henry was quiet for the first part of the ride. Finally, he spoke. "Walt, now that you've heard my story from beginning to end, I want your opinion. Am I a bad man? Am I evil?"

From what I knew as an armchair psychologist, him just asking that question was a pretty good indication that the man had a conscience and was suffering from a severe case of guilt.

"No, Henry, I don't think you're evil," I replied. "I think that circumstances put you and your family in a horrible situation. I can't begin to imagine what you were feeling. I think that you made some choices that were certainly questionable, but who's to say what anyone might have done if they were in your shoes. The bottom line for me is that you didn't pull that trigger and you've done everything in your power to make things right."

"Thank you for that," he replied.

I could tell that he still wasn't convinced.

We pulled into the driveway of the fake safe house without incident. I heaved a sigh of relief as I turned off the engine.

The fake Marsha met us at the door and gave Henry a big hug. If Jaeger was watching, I hoped the performance was convincing.

We hunkered down inside the house, away from doors and windows, waiting for the assault that we hoped would be coming. Mark's men, concealed throughout the neighborhood, would be ready to pounce once the attack had begun.

Two hours had passed and Jaeger was a no-show.

We were all stiff and cramped from crouching behind the big overstuffed furniture that we hoped would protect us from the hail of bullets that never came.

Mark was discouraged. "I can't believe that he hasn't hit us. Do you think something tipped him off?"

I was at a loss for words. I wanted this thing to be over. The waiting and uncertainty, knowing that a cold-blooded killer was out there, was weighing on us all.

"Let me check with my men," Mark said, "and if they've seen nothing, we'll call it a night."

After speaking with each of his posted sentries, Mark said, "Nothing! Quiet as a grave yard out there."

I wished that Mark could have come up with a different simile.

"I'll drive Henry to the Anderson house," I said. "That way you can wrap things up here."

"Great!" Mark said. "Give me a call after you've dropped him off so I'll know everyone is safe."

We pulled up in front of the Anderson house. The lights were on inside.

"Looks like they waited up for you," I said. "I'll walk you to the door and then give Mark a call."

When I reached into my pocket and pulled out my cell phone, I realized that I hadn't powered it back on after the broadcast. The anchor was adamant about not being interrupted by an errant call, so I had turned it completely off.

We were almost to the door when my phone powered up. It immediately rang and I saw Willie's smiling face on the screen.

I was about to answer when I noticed that the wood on the door jam had been splintered.

I hit the 'ignore' button, shoved the phone in my pocket and drew my pistol.

"Something's wrong here," I whispered. "Stay behind me."

We had just stepped onto the porch when I felt the cold steel of a gun barrel pressed against my back.

"I'll take that, cop," the skinhead said, grabbing my gun.

Two more skinheads emerged from inside.

"Jaeger!" Henry exclaimed. "Where's my family? What have you done with them?"

"Yes, Henry, it's me," Jaeger said with a snarl. "Your family is safe --- for now. But not for long. I told you what would happen if you crossed me. First I'll do the old man, then his wife, then Marsha. Little Billy will get to see his mommy die. Then I'll do the kid. You'll get to see them all die before I finish you off very slowly. I'll do the old cop last. That way he can see what happens when the law tries to screw around with the Brotherhood."

Then he turned to me. "Did you really think that I would fall for your pathetic little ruse?"

Under the circumstances, I thought it best not to speak.

"What's the matter? Cat got your tongue? Maybe I should just cut it out of your mouth right now!"

He looked at his watch. "Naw, plenty of time for that later. Let's get Henry to his family. I've been looking forward to this reunion for a long time."

Jaeger pushed us into an SUV.

As we drove across town, I thought about how I was going to call Maggie and tell her that I was okay and on the way home, right after I gave Mark the 'all clear'.

It was beginning to look like I wouldn't be making that call.

Willie, Louie and Darius were in the Caddy in the alley behind the old Payday Loan store.

"Give Walt another try," Louie said.

Willie dialed the number, but as before, the call went to voice mail. He shook his head.

"Then let's do dis," Louie said. "Darius, go see if you can pick dat lock on de back door."

He slipped out and was back a minute later.

"Piece of cake."

"Good," Louie replied, handing Darius a snub-nosed .38. "Den take dis an' we be ready to go."

"Uncle Louie!" Darius protested, "You know I don't do no guns!"

"I respect dat, son, but sometimes you jus' gotta do what you gotta do. I promise I won't tell your granny."

The three of them slipped out of the car.

Darius went to work with his lock picks and a few minutes later, they heard the 'click'.

"Okay, Willie," Louie said. "Grab yo' pizzas and do yo' thing. Be seein' you inside."

Willie went back to the Caddy and retrieved three large pizza boxes out of the back seat.

He carried the steaming boxes to the front door and knocked.

"Who's there!" a voice called from inside.

"Pizza guy!" Willie shouted through the door.

"I got yo' delivery."

"Didn't order no pizza," the voice said.

"Well somebody did," Willie replied, "and dis is de address dey give me."

The door opened a crack and the cheesy smell drifted inside.

"Jocco! It's pizza all right! Maybe Jaeger ordered it for us."

"Let 'em in," Jocco ordered.

Willie stepped into the room and saw Henry's family huddled together in the corner.

"Just put them on the table," the first man said.

Willie did as he was ordered and then looked at the ticket.

"Dat'll be $27.50," he said.

"Ain't got that much. Jocco! You got some money?"

"A little," Jocco replied. "Get out your wallets and let's get this guy out of here."

As the three of them huddled in the middle of the room, peering into their wallets, Louie and Darius stepped in from the back of the building with their weapons drawn.

"Don't forget to give the guy a tip," Louie said.

"Jocco started to go for his gun, but Louie waved his automatic menacingly. "I wouldn't do dat, Skinhead. Willie, tie up dese jokers den we can all have some pizza."

Jaeger pulled to the curb near an old storefront on Troost. At that hour, it was the only building on the block with lights glowing inside.

Henry and I were ordered out of the car and stood waiting with guns at our backs while Jaeger knocked.

When no one answered, Jaeger kicked the door. "Shit! Where are those idiots?"

He motioned to one of his buddies, "Unlock it."

When we were inside, Henry's family was lined up against the far wall.

The minute we walked in the door, Billy broke away from his mother and ran to Henry grabbing him around the knees.

"Dad!"

Jaeger looked around the room. "Jocco! Where in the hell are you?" he screamed.

"Jocko's a little tied up right now," Louie said, as he, Willie and Darius stepped into the room with guns drawn.

"Well, well," Jaeger said with a sneer. "Looks like we've got a black posse here. You've got guns and we've got guns. Looks like a Mexican standoff."

"Ironic," I said. "Mexicans and blacks. Two of your favorite groups!"

"Shut up old man!" my captor said, giving me

a whack on the head.

"We definitely have a problem here," Jaeger said. "It looks like people are going to die here tonight. I promise you that if one shot is fired, the first person to die will be this coward in front of me. I promised Henry that if he crossed me, he would pay. I think it might just be time to collect."

"You leave my Dad alone!" Billy shouted, and kicked Jaeger savagely in the shin.

At that moment, all hell broke loose.

Jaeger screamed and lowered the pistol to little Billy who was wailing away at his leg.

Henry grabbed Jaeger's arm and the two of them rolled onto the floor.

At that instant, I dropped to the ground. I heard the blasts from Willie and Louie's guns and the two Skinheads crumpled around me.

Henry and Jaeger were locked in each other's arms, each desperately trying to gain control of the gun.

I was about to leap into the fray, when the gun went off.

Everyone held their breath as the two lay motionless.

Finally, Henry pushed Jaegers' lifeless body aside and laid the gun on the floor.

Billy grabbed his father around the neck and cried.

Some might call it fate. Some might call it karma.

Henry Martin had indeed become an assassin.

EPILOGUE

I heard Louie's old Cadillac pull way from the alley just as Mark Davenport and his men entered the old storefront.

"Jesus, Walt!" he exclaimed as once again he looked at the carnage strewn around the room. "Don't tell me you did all this single-handed."

"Actually, I didn't do any of it," I replied. "I had some help, but they thought there might be less red tape if they left and I just filled in the blanks."

"I don't suppose that it was the same 'help' that assisted you in wrapping up the Vipers?"

"It might have been."

Mark just shook his head. "If they keep this up, we may have to give them a badge."

"I think they'd rather remain anonymous," I replied. "By the way, how did you find us?"

"GPS on your phone," he replied. "When I didn't hear from you, I tried to call my man at the Anderson safe house. When he didn't answer, I figured something had gone sour. I had the office run a trace on your phone and followed you here."

He looked at the body in the middle of the floor. "Jaeger?"

I nodded. "When the coroner does the autopsy, he's going to find some nasty bruises on the guy's shins courtesy of little Billy. I don't know how all of this would have come down if the kid hadn't attacked him."

"So it was Billy that may have prevented

Henry from shooting the president and Billy that led the attack on the Skinheads. Maybe Billy is the one that should be shaking the president's hand."

"I think I remember something I heard from Pastor Bob one day. Something about 'a little child shall lead them'. Anyway, rather than shaking the president's hand, I'm pretty sure that Billy would rather have his Dad back. Any chance of that?'

"I'll see what I can do," Mark said with a knowing smile.

It was several days before everything was sorted out and all the i's dotted and t's crossed on the voluminous report that chronicled the failed assassination attempt on the president.

True to his word, Mark had spoken to the president about amnesty for Henry. Truth be told, all he was actually guilty of was conspiracy, and in one sense, if it were a cop that had been sent undercover to do the things that Henry did, exposing two very dangerous groups, he would have been hailed a hero.

Unfortunately, the only two people that knew which powerful interests had financed the attempt were Brant Jaeger and Terrance Cobb. Since Jaeger was dead and Cobb was in the wind, Henry and his family were still in jeopardy.

All five of them were placed in witness protection. Since both of the family homes had been destroyed along with all their possessions, Henry was allowed to keep the money in the offshore account to help finance his new life.

Somewhere out there in our great land, a young family, having overcome tremendous obstacles, is getting an opportunity to rebuild their lives, and isn't that what America is all about?

As I reflected on my last two cases, I couldn't help but wonder what had instilled the hate that I had witnessed in the Vipers and the Aryan Brotherhood.

One of my favorite musicals is *South Pacific* and perhaps one of the hardest hitting scenes is when Philadelphia born Lieutenant Cable falls in love with Liat, a Tonkinese girl, but can't commit to her.

The words of his song speak volumes about the human condition.

You've got to be taught to hate and fear. You've got to be taught from year to year.
It's got to be drummed in your dear little ear. Yes, you've got to be carefully taught.

You've got to be taught to be afraid, of people whose eyes are oddly made
And people whose skin is a different shade. Yes, you've got to be carefully taught!

Rashon Rippe and Brant Jaeger had been carefully taught, and the hate that festered inside them touched the lives of countless people.

How does one explain why men such as these

can wage war on people just because they are different, and then on the other hand, there's Louie and Willie, two black men that were willing to lay their lives on the line for an old white cop.

What is the thing that keeps one man from pulling a trigger while another man can take a life without regret or remorse?

The dictionary tells us that conscience is an aptitude, faculty, intuition or judgment that distinguishes right from wrong.

The experts tell us that somehow, that faculty is absent in sociopaths like Brant Jaeger.

Unfortunately, there are thousands more like him walking our streets and endangering the lives of innocent people.

When those without a conscience tip the scales of justice, the Lady with the blindfold needs brave men to come forward to balance those scales.

My name is Walt Williams and that's why I'm a cop!

****

Author's Note

As the author of the Lady Justice series, my main goal has been to bring a smile to my reader's face and a bit of laughter into their lives.

Nevertheless, some of Walt's fictional adventures have taken him face-to-face with some very real but also very controversial topics.

In *Lady Justice and Dr. Death*, it was euthanasia; in *Lady Justice and the Sting*, it was the collusion between the FDA, corrupt politicians and the pharmaceutical giants; in *Lady Justice and the Watchers*, it was government conspiracies and in *Lady Justice and the Candidate*, it was our political system.

In this latest installment, *Lady Justice and the Assassin*, Walt finds himself pitted against foes filled with hate and racial bigotry.

It is my hope that these controversial subjects, presented in the context of Walt's improbable exploits, will stimulate thought along with the lighter side.

I, like Walt, often find myself struggling with how the human moral compass can get so 'out of whack', but also like Walt, I have faith in the basic goodness inside each of us and a belief that Lady Justice will prevail.

ABOUT THE AUTHOR

Award-winning author, Robert Thornhill, began writing at the age of sixty-six, and in three short years has penned thirteen novels in the Lady Justice mystery/comedy series, the seven volume Rainbow Road series of chapter books for children, a cookbook and a mini-autobiography.

The fifth, sixth, seventh and ninth novels in his Lady Justice series, *Lady Justice and the Sting, Lady Justice and Dr. Death, Lady Justice and the Vigilante* and *Lady Justice and the Candidate* won the Pinnacle Achievement Award from the National Association of Book Entrepreneurs as the best mystery novels in 2011 and 2012.

Robert holds a master's degree in psychology, but his wit and insight come from his varied occupations including thirty years as a real estate broker.

He lives with his wife, Peg, in Independence, Mo.

LADY JUSTICE TAKES A C.R.A.P.
City Retiree Action Patrol
Third Edition

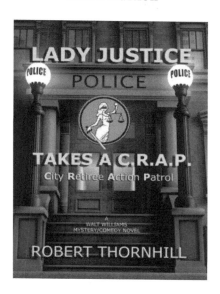

This is where it all began.

See how sixty-five year old Walt Williams became a cop and started the City Retiree Action Patrol.

Meet Maggie, Willie, Mary and the Professor, Walt's sidekicks in all of the Lady Justice novels.

Laugh out loud as Walt and his band of Senior Scrappers capture the Realtor Rapist and take down the Russian Mob.

http://booksbybob.com/lady-justice-takes-a-crap-3rd_383.html

LADY JUSTICE AND THE LOST TAPES

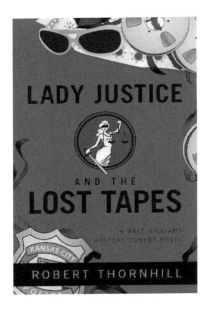

In *Lady Justice and the Lost Tapes*, Walt and his band of scrappy seniors continue their battle against the forces of evil.

When an entire eastside Kansas City neighborhood is terrorized by the mob, Walt must go undercover to solve the case.

Later, the amazing discovery of a previously unknown recording session of a deceased rock 'n' roll idol stuns the music industry.

http://booksbybob.com/lady-justice-and-the-lost-tapes_307.html

LADY JUSTICE GETS LEI'D

In *Lady Justice Gets Lei'd*, Walt and Maggie plan a romantic honeymoon on the beautiful Hawaiian Islands, but ancient artifacts discovered in a cave in a dormant volcano and a surprising revelation about Maggie's past, lead our lovers into the hands of Hawaiian zealots.

http://booksbybob.com/lady-justice-gets-leid_309.html

LADY JUSTICE AND THE
AVENGING ANGELS

Lady Justice has unwittingly entered a religious war.

Who better to fight for her than Walt Williams?

The Avenging Angels believe that it's their job to rain fire and brimstone on Kansas City, their Sodom and Gomorrah.

In this compelling addition to the Lady Justice series, Robert Thornhill brings back all the characters readers have come to love for more hilarity and higher stakes.

You'll laugh and be on the edge of your seat until the big finish.

Don't miss *Lady Justice and the Avenging Angels!*

http://booksbybob.com/lady-justice-and-the-avenging-angels_336.html

LADY JUSTICE AND THE STING

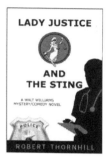

BEST NEW MYSTERY NOVEL ---WINTER 2012

National Association of Book Entrepreneurs

In *Lady Justice and the Sting*, a holistic physician is murdered and Walt becomes entangled in the high-powered world of pharmaceutical giants and corrupt politicians.

Maggie, Ox Willie, Mary and all your favorite characters are back to help Walt bring the criminals to justice in the most unorthodox ways.

A dead-serious mystery with hilarious twists!
http://booksbybob.com/lady-justice-and-the-sting_348.html

LADY JUSTICE AND DR. DEATH

BEST NEW MYSTERY NOVEL --- FALL 2011

National Association of Book Entrepreneurs

In *Lady Justice and Dr. Death*, a series of terminally ill patients are found dead under circumstances that point to a new Dr. Death practicing euthanasia in the Kansas City area.

Walt and his entourage of scrappy seniors are dragged into the 'right-to-die-with-dignity' controversy.

The mystery provides a light-hearted look at this explosive topic and death in general.

You may see end-of-life issues in a whole new light after reading *Lady Justice and Dr. Death*! http://booksbybob.com/lady-justice-and-dr-death_351.html

LADY JUSTICE AND THE VIGILANTE

BEST NEW MYSTERY NOVEL – SUMMER 2012

National Association of Book Entrepreneurs

A vigilante is stalking the streets of Kansas City administering his own brand of justice when the justice system fails.

Criminals are being executed right under the noses of the police department.

A new recruit to the City Retiree Action Patrol steps up to help Walt and Ox bring an end to his reign of terror.

But not everyone wants the vigilante stopped. His bold reprisals against the criminal element have inspired the average citizen to take up arms and defend themselves.

As the body count mounts, public opinion is split.

Is it justice or is it murder?

A moral dilemma that will leave you laughing and weeping!

http://booksbybob.com/lady-justice-and-the-vigilante_362.html

LADY JUSTICE AND THE WATCHERS

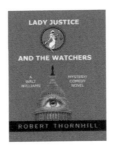

Suzanne Collins wrote *The Hunger Games*, Aldous Huxley wrote *Brave New World* and George Orwell wrote *1984*.

All three novels were about dystopian societies of the future.

In *Lady Justice and the Watchers*, Walt sees the world we live in today through the eyes of a group who call themselves 'The Watchers'.

Oscar Levant said that there's a fine line between genius and insanity.

After reading *Lady Justice and the Watchers*, you may realize as Walt did that there's also a fine line separating the life of freedom that we enjoy today and the totalitarian society envisioned in these classic novels.

Quietly and without fanfare, powerful interests have instituted policies that have eroded our privacy, health and individual freedoms.

Is the dystopian society still a thing of the distant future or is it with us now disguised as a wolf in sheep's clothing?

http://booksbybob.com/lady-justice-and-the-watchers_365.html

LADY JUSTICE AND THE CANDIDATE

BEST NEW MYSTERY NOVEL – FALL 2012

National Association of Book Entrepreneurs

Will American politics always be dominated by the two major political parties or are voters longing for an Independent candidate to challenge the establishment?

Everyone thought that the slate of candidates for the presidential election had been set until Benjamin Franklin Foster came on the scene capturing the hearts of American voters with his message of change and reform.

Powerful interests intent on preserving the status quo with their bought-and-paid-for politicians were determined to take Ben Foster out of the race.

The Secret Service comes up with a quirky plan to protect the Candidate and strike a blow for Lady Justice.

Join Walt on the campaign trail for an adventure full of surprises, mystery, intrigue and laughs!

http://booksbybob.com/lady-justice-and-the-candidate_367.html

LADY JUSTICE
AND THE
BOOK CLUB MURDERS

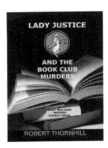

Members of the Midtown Book Club are found murdered.

It is just the beginning of a series of deaths that lead Walt and Ox into the twisted world of a serial killer.

In the late 1960's, the Zodiac Killer claimed to have killed 37 people and was never caught --- the perfect crime.

Oscar Roach, dreamed of being the next serial killer to commit the perfect crime.

He left a calling card with each of his victims --- a mystery novel, resting in their blood-soaked hands.

The media dubbed him 'The Librarian'.

Walt and the Kansas City Police are baffled by the cunning of this vicious killer and fear that he has indeed committed the perfect crime.

Or did he?

Walt and his wacky senior cohorts prove, once again, that life goes on in spite of the carnage around them.

The perfect blend of murder, mayhem and merriment.

http://booksbybob.com/lady-justice-and-the-book-club-murders_370.html

LADY JUSTICE
AND THE
CRUISE SHIP MURDERS

Ox and Judy are off to Alaska on a honeymoon cruise and invite Walt and Maggie to tag along.

Their peaceful plans are soon shipwrecked by the murder of two fellow passengers.

The murders appear to be linked to a century-old legend involving a cache of gold stolen from a prospector and buried by two thieves.

Their seven-day cruise is spent hunting for the gold and eluding the modern day thieves intent on possessing it at any cost.

Another nail-biting mystery that will have you on the edge of your seat one minute and laughing out loud the next.

http://booksbybob.com/lady-justice-and-the-cruise-ship-murders_373.html

LADY JUSTICE
AND THE
CLASS REUNION

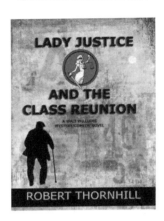

For most people, a 50th class reunion is a time to party and renew old acquaintances, but Walt Williams isn't an ordinary guy --- he's a cop, and trouble seems to follow him everywhere he goes.

The Mexican drug cartel is recruiting young Latino girls as drug mules and the Kansas City Police have hit a brick wall until Walt is given a lead by an old classmate.

Even then, it takes three unlikely heroes from the Whispering Hills Retirement Village to help Walt and Ox end the cartel's reign of terror.

Join Walt in a class reunion filled with mystery, intrigue, jealousy and a belly-full of laughs! http://booksbybob.com/lady-justice-and-the-class-reunion_387.html

WOLVES IN SHEEP'S CLOTHING

In August of 2011, I completed the fifth novel in the *Lady Justice* mystery/comedy series, *Lady Justice And The Sting*.

As I always do, I sent copies of the completed manuscript to several friends and acquaintances for their feedback and comments before sending the manuscript to the publisher.

Since the plot involved a holistic physician, I sent a copy to Dr. Edward Pearson in Florida.

Dr. Pearson loved the premise of the book and the style of writing, particularly as it related to alternative healthcare, natural products and Walt's transformation into a healthier lifestyle.

In subsequent conversations, Dr. Pearson shared that he had been looking for a book that he could share with his patients, colleagues and peers that would spread his message in a format that would capture their imagination and their hearts.

The Sting was very close to what he had been looking for and he made the suggestion that maybe we could work together to produce just the right book.

As I reflected on this idea, I realized that Walt's skirmishes with pharmaceutical companies, corrupt politicians, doctors, nurses, hospitals, bodily afflictions and a healthier lifestyle were not confined to just *The Sting*, but were scattered throughout all six of the *Lady Justice* mystery/comedy novels.

Using *The Sting* as the basis of the new book, I went through the manuscripts of the other five *Lady Justice* novels and pulled out chapters and vignettes that fleshed out the story of Walt's medical adventures.

Thus, *Wolves In Sheep's Clothing* was born.

Dr. Pearson is currently using *Wolves* in conjunction with his New Medicine Foundation to help spread the word about healthcare alternatives.

New Medicine Foundation
Dr. Edward W. Pearson, MD, ABIHM
http://newmedicinefoundation.com

RAINBOW ROAD
CHAPTER BOOKS FOR CHILDREN
AGES 5 – 10

Super Secrets of Rainbow Road

Super Powers of Rainbow Road

Hawaiian Rainbows

Patriotic Rainbows

Sports Heroes of Rainbow Road

Ghosts and Goblins of Rainbow Road

Christmas Crooks of Rainbow Road

http://booksbybob.com/childrens-books-special-offer_316.html

5220530R00120

Made in the USA
San Bernardino, CA
30 October 2013